D1525117

The Driftwood Inn

Cape Canaveral North, book 1

Amy Ashley

Timothy Lane Press

Contents

Chapter One

Miranda Cole gazed into the lobby of her B&B, The Driftwood Inn, with a sense of accomplishment. She had started this sole endeavor almost fifteen years ago and was never sorry she'd taken the plunge.

Her husband, Bill, had been supportive all those years ago when she started her Driftwood Inn business, but lately ... not so much. Or perhaps his attitude was simply that he didn't think about her bed-and-breakfast as much of a business anymore. If he ever had.

He hadn't ever participated in the day-to-day running of it. He'd also never contributed financially to her business. Not one thin dime. But that was okay, because she could say she'd built this thriving bed-and-breakfast all on her own. She'd prospered because of her own good sense, plus a healthy amount of grit and determination.

When she started out, she'd gotten a business loan along with a business account at their bank. However, the Driftwood Inn bed-and-breakfast was in her name only.

Bill was listed as the death beneficiary for twenty percent if there was any left after paying all the Driftwood Inn's debts. The other eighty percent was to be divided equally among their four children. Miranda liked equality. She spent so much time when the kids were little buying four of everything it was hard not to do it now, even though her children were all grown and gone.

Perhaps Bill didn't care about her business anymore, or maybe he never had, really, with the exception that now The Driftwood Inn was paying their bills and not the income from *his* job. That had changed only in the last five to eight years.

Bill's extreme pride of late would never allow him to congratulate her for being the breadwinner in their small family. Nor would he ever even acknowledge that the hard work she'd invested in the Inn for a decade and a half had all been worth the endless effort she'd put into this place. Or perhaps he felt it was *her* turn to pay their bills for a change, since he'd done it for so long before she was solvent in her business.

Back when she started, while he'd never discouraged her from wanting to open an Inn, he'd also made it a point to ensure that her business wasn't connected to their combined income, especially with regard to their taxes. Lately, she was grateful for that, too, even though she'd been a little hurt back then of his insistence that they keep their financial lives separate.

It was as though Bill believed she'd fail even

before she started and he didn't want to put everything—or, really, anything—on the line. He'd never said that, of course, but that was how she'd felt all those years ago. His rule of letting her go it all alone in her business had made a few things tougher for her for a while, but she'd come through and been successful anyway. Now she felt vindicated to have basically created this prosperous business all by her lonesome.

She was truly grateful that her business was still viable, especially now, since Bill had changed so dramatically in the past few years, and in so many ways.

His appearance, his attitude and his day-to-day life was so altered from when they'd married, she barely recognized him. However, that was a worry for another day. She shook off her concern for her husband's personality change and focused back on her bed-and-breakfast. It gave her much more satisfaction than her stormy, silent marriage of late.

Miranda took another long, prideful look around and nodded with supreme satisfaction at a job well done. She closed her eyes and sent up a little prayer of gratitude, also requesting a blessing for her continued success.

She headed to the registration desk, since it was near the end of the day. She'd gotten all of her chores done. First she'd taken care of setting up tomorrow's breakfast buffet. Then, she'd talked to the trio of housekeepers who took care of all the daily room cleaning. She got her weekly update from them, asked if they had all they needed and addressed any and all concerns. She was told things were in very good shape. No complaints.

Everything was running smoothly. Just the way she liked it.

Miranda breathed a sigh of relief that she had such a great staff to help her with the Driftwood Inn, especially her cleaning crew. Good housekeepers were hard to find and Miranda did her best to keep hers happy.

Darby Anders, the Driftwood Inn's day manager, would be finishing up and getting ready to go home. She also handled any personnel issues for the staff, such as earnings distribution and a days off calendar. On top of that, she managed the account books and a multitude of other things for the Driftwood Inn. Darby was truly Miranda's right arm in this B&B business.

Poor Darby had a tragic past. One day long ago, Miranda had taken a risk and hired her at the start of her fledgling business. Even though Darby didn't have proof of her credentials—just her word that she'd work hard and never give her any trouble—Miranda hired her on a gut feeling that hadn't let her down.

Darby had been more than qualified to do the job. She did more than required, in fact. And as promised, she'd never given Miranda any trouble at all.

Hiring Darby turned out to be the best decision Miranda ever made. Together they were a great team. Darby had never forgotten the favor. Even all these years later, she acted as though Miranda had saved her life and expressed her gratitude regularly.

Miranda was the one who was grateful. She didn't know how things would have gone in this business without Darby at her side.

Miranda always checked in with Darby for a regular report at the end of the day and also to catch up in general. Lately, things at the Driftwood Inn had been pretty good.

Not perfect, but they were profitable enough to make ends meet and pay everyone's salary. With the income from the Driftwood Inn, Miranda ran the business, paid all her personal bills and even had enough left over to have a growing savings account. Best of all, they had a steady flow of regular guests with plans to visit annually, adding to her continued success.

In a beach town with lots of competition, she was lucky to be in better shape than most along the sandy beach of Cape Canaveral North.

Although Cape Canaveral Beach to the south had quite a few more inns along that section of the coast, Cape Canaveral North was a bit smaller and there were not as many inns located directly on the water. Miranda wasn't even sure where the exact dividing line between the two communities was, but there was a quieter mood in the northern area versus their neighbors to the south.

Cape Canaveral North's beach area had more foliage and less overall traffic. Miranda didn't have hard-core facts on her side, it was more of a feeling. Or perhaps she just enjoyed her corner of the world more and that was reflected in her attitude about her surroundings.

Her best friend, Roberta Pierce, used to live in Cape Canaveral Beach, down the way, before she and her husband retired from the innkeeping business and moved to Key West five years or so ago.

But after her husband, Charlie, died more than a year ago, Roberta had come back up to her old stomping grounds to help her daughter, Beth, at the Lighthouse Inn. There had been rumors of some trouble with Beth's husband, resulting in a rather public, drama-filled, blowup that led to their divorce, but Miranda hadn't heard the whole story yet from any reliable sources.

One day she and Roberta would have a chat to catch up on all things personal. Until they did, things seemed to be running smoothly at the Lighthouse Inn these days.

Over the years, Roberta and Miranda had helped each other out whenever possible. Miranda had been afraid the competition would ruin their friendship. If anything, the relationship was made stronger by their common interests and being confidants and also giving them each a back channel rescue if they needed help.

Recently, Miranda's daughter, Zoe, had married Roberta's son, Evan Pierce. That was an amazingly happy day. While she and Roberta had wanted to plan a big wedding together if their children ever fell in love and set a wedding date, Zoe and Evan had eloped, striking that plan from day one.

Miranda wasn't surprised by the action, given she knew how Zoe felt about big weddings. It turned out Roberta wasn't particularly bothered by the elopement, either, since she was perpetually worried that her son would never marry at all, so any marriage was welcome.

While the big dream wedding uniting their families didn't happen, they didn't complain. Together the four of them decided that the two moms could plan a nice reception for them later in the summer. Letting go of their dream of a big wedding was easy for Miranda and Roberta, since they secretly planned to have a baby shower extravaganza once they became expectant grandmas.

She and Roberta couldn't wait, even though their kids had told them it would be quite a while before they planned to become parents, throwing water on any immediate baby party plans. Even so, Miranda thought it was great to have Roberta as official family, since they'd been unofficial family for so many years.

The season here along the central East Coast truly started for the Driftwood Inn during March, often with a bunch of young, college-aged spring break guests for that month and well into April, sometimes for another whole month.

Then there were just average vacation guests without children until mid-summer, when the family vacationers came non-stop until mid- to late August. Miranda was rarely without a full or nearly full B&B throughout the summer months.

In the past two or three years, she would have been able to accommodate up to half a dozen or more guests if she'd had more rooms. That was the reason behind her coming expansion plan to add half a dozen more rooms to her establishment.

She'd let all her regular guests know the renovation work was coming. So far, no one had backed out, telling her that as long as the hammers were flying while they were out at the beach and not at night, they didn't care. She felt she could make that promise, as she didn't want hammers flying at night, either.

From the first part of April until hopefully mid-December, there would be a big construction project on the north side of the Inn, adding more rooms and a very nice lower-level common room especially designed with her annual Christmas celebration in mind.

It was why she was hoping and praying that the construction would be completed in time for the annual Christmas party she hosted for family, friends and special guests. This year would be her official fifteenth year in business. Miranda wanted to be able to celebrate as usual, of course, but also note the fifteen-year mark in a special way—for example, in a spiffy, brand new common room designed for the occasion.

Starting this year, or once the expansion was finished, the party would be held in the new common area of the addition to the Driftwood Inn. She had the room designed for that singular purpose in mind, although the area would be used for many other things throughout the year.

Miranda couldn't wait until construction was completed, and it hadn't even started yet. She smiled to herself at the foolish notion.

Theo Jackson was her construction guy. He told her it would be close, trying to get finished by her party deadline, but promised to do his best to make her Christmas wish come true. She knew he'd try his hardest. Theo was not only a good man, he was an excellent worker and if he promised to do his best, Miranda could be assured he would do everything within his power to complete the extension to the Driftwood Inn by the first week of December.

Miranda paused at the doorway to the Inn's entry and leaned one shoulder against the wall. Glancing around the lobby, she catalogued all the changes she'd made in the last fourteen-plus years. Was there a surface she hadn't touched? Probably not.

As she pondered fourteen-plus years' worth of changes, a sudden and dread-filled feeling raced through her, from head to heart to belly to toes and up again. She took a couple of steps back and sat down hard on a bench seat in the hallway that led from the kitchen to the lobby, grateful it was there or she would have collapsed to the floor.

What on Earth was that?

Chapter Two

Miranda closed her eyes and focused on breathing as the dread-filled feeling slowly passed. She sensed very strongly that something was coming. Something big. The dread-filled part meant it was likely not a good thing, though she couldn't be certain.

Whatever it was, something was on its way. Did it have something to do with the construction that was about to begin? Her stormy marriage? Something she didn't know about yet? She wasn't sure and couldn't tell.

Miranda hadn't had a feeling like this since she'd been a little kid.

Back then, her twin sister Maribelle had broken her collarbone after falling off her bicycle in the street. Miranda had been across town at her piano lesson when a similar feeling of *something* had swooped through her.

She'd been in the middle of a poor rendition of Chopsticks when a feeling of dread hit her so hard and so fast, she practically fell off the piano bench. She sat, fingers poised ever so carefully over the piano keys, getting ready to play the tune again, to do better, then whatever it was suddenly forced her hands to slam down, rendering a nightmarish sound only heard in horror movies.

Mrs. Collins, her piano teacher, had been so alarmed, she lurched backward, almost toppling them both off the piano bench. Miranda burst into tears. The kind woman quickly fetched Miranda a glass of water and made her lay down on the sofa. The phone rang a few minutes later with the news that her parents were rushing Maribelle to the hospital and would pick Miranda up late from her piano lesson.

She'd never been a superstitious person and wasn't into any woo-woo mystical stuff like her twin sister Maribelle was, but Miranda was willing to admit that sometimes unexplainable things happened.

Did this feeling mean her sister was in trouble? That would be nothing new. No. Miranda didn't think this was related to her sister. Just the same, she made a mental note to call Maribelle later. Just to make sure.

She rubbed her palms up and down her arms to get rid of the bad feeling, stood up and continued out to the registration desk in the lobby.

"Hi, Miranda. I'm glad you're here," Darby said. "It's been a really great day so far. I'm dying to tell you about it." Darby grinned from ear to ear and looked like she was about to leap into the air and cheer.

Miranda cleared her throat and forced herself to smile at Darby's exuberance. "Has it? Tell me all."

"Well, we are currently at eighty percent occupancy. Isn't that awesome?"

Miranda was shocked. "Really? How did that happen?"

Darby looked as smug as a Cheshire cat and leaned forward as if about to impart all the secrets of the world. "Well, this guy came in earlier with his large family of six, including his mother, and rented four rooms. Four! Can you believe it?"

"Wow. Awesome. Just a walk-in? That's amazing."

"Yes, so amazing," the other woman said, her expression gleeful. The look on Darby's face told her there was also a story.

She continued, "It seems that the Pineapple Cove Inn either lost or messed up their reservations, even though they made them months ago. Anyway, the Pineapple Cove Inn could only provide two rooms on short notice."

"Interesting. I wonder how they messed it up." Miranda wasn't a fan of the owners of the Pineapple Cove Inn, but didn't wish them ill.

"I have a theory." Darby, eyes flashing, was well into storytelling mode by now.

"Tell me."

Darby leaned even closer and lowered her voice. "Well, rumor has it that the Pineapple Cove Inn has been turned over to the eldest and only son of the owners. He has been making all sorts of changes to update things, including a new and clearly very confusing reservation system. He's also changed pretty much everything from the sheets to the cleansers they use, making the long-time staff *very* unhappy, as well."

Miranda wondered how Darby came by all this juicy information, but figured if the Pine-apple Cove Inn's new management had instituted so much change all at once, it would be a miracle if it didn't anger the staff. They likely started looking for new jobs that came with less hassle, and once that occurred, the rumors would start churning through the local gossip mill automatically.

"Change is hard," Miranda said. But she was also thinking more about Darby's theory regarding the changes at the Pineapple Cove Inn and the next generation of innkeepers. She had it in mind to do the same thing with the Driftwood Inn by pass-ing her business on to her children, especially Zoe. However, she'd certainly impress upon her kids the importance of not ruining everything with lots of changes all at once.

"I hear the son has shaken things up quite a bit," Darby continued. "And as such, many of the longtime staffers started looking elsewhere for work. Apparently, when the son heard about it, he just fired everyone, told them they were paid too much anyway and replaced the lot of them with unskilled high school students and others with no experience in the hotel business, but who would work cheap, even if they didn't know what they were doing. And clearly they don't."

"Sounds like it," Miranda said. "That isn't very good for business, if you ask me."

"I agree. Personally, I think's it's foolish to anger the staff and then fire them when they clearly know more about the business than the new owner and are only trying to ensure they have a good job. I guess the son doesn't see it that way."

"Wow. That's quite a story," Miranda said to Darby. Quickly, she tried to figure out how this would impact her business. In the short term, it was awesome to be at an eighty percent capacity. She felt somewhat sorry for the Pineapple Cove Inn, but not too bad.

They had been Miranda's biggest competition here on the north side of Cape Canaveral Beach. And the owners had been a bit snotty to her on more than one occasion, when they certainly didn't have to be. Sounded like the son was cut from the same cloth.

"Anyway," Darby continued, "The Thorne family came here all the way from Montana. The father was so mad at the Pineapple Cove Inn's incompetence, as he called it, that he walked out and drove down the street until he saw our place and called the registration desk from his car out in the front parking lot area. I could hear crying and complaining in the background during the whole call until I told them we had plenty of rooms to accommodate him and his whole family."

Miranda laughed. "Well, I'm glad we had

enough rooms for them all."

"Me, too. So, I put them all in the north hallway. We only have two prepared rooms left now."

"That's truly amazing." Miranda felt unsettled. Was this the cause of the weird feeling she'd had? Maybe. Hopefully. She mentally shook off that previous feeling of anxiousness and patted Darby on the back. "Good job, Darby."

"Thanks. It feels good to help someone out when they've lost hope. And in my humble opinion, no one should lose hope while on their only annual vacation."

"I agree. I'm so glad we were able to step up and help them out. So, how much did you charge for the rooms? Did you give them a discount?" Miranda hoped they hadn't had to take too much of a cut in the rate. She didn't think her prices were unreasonable and she certainly wasn't rigid, especially when several rooms were rented by one party. All the same, she did have bills to pay.

Darby winked. "Didn't have to give him a discount. He asked if he could get the four rooms for an amount that was almost fifteen percent higher than we would have normally charged. I told him we could do that and even knocked off five percent to be friendly once he came in and handed me his credit card. He acted like I'd handed him a treasure trove. You should have seen the grin light up his face. Gave me goosebumps to make him so happy. Plus, the guy really sounded relieved. First, at finding a place, and second, that it didn't cost him double what he'd been prepared to pay."

"I'll bet. Instead of good job, I say excellent job, Darby, as usual. And now we know what the new room rates at the Pineapple Cove Inn are, meaning we could raise our official rates by five to ten per cent and still not be higher than the Pineapple Cove Inn."

"Exactly what I thought. And best of all, the Thorne family are staying for ten days." She clapped her hands in glee. "I mean, that's awesome, right?"

Miranda clapped her hands in glee, too, but not as loudly.

Darby said, "Now I can retire early, too."

"Don't you dare. I need you."

She just laughed and shook her head. "I'm not leaving, Miranda. I love this job. I picture us as decrepit old ladies still roaming around here in fifty years having walker races."

Miranda laughed out loud at Darby's description of their elder years. "I can't tell you how glad I am to hear that. I'll even let you win the walker race every so often."

Darby laughed, too, but soon they got back down to business. They went over the day's schedule and the menu for the next week. She told Darby about the meeting she'd had with the housekeepers and that there were no current issues to be resolved. They also discussed the upcoming renovation.

"I know it's going to be a bit taxing for you,

Darby. Hopefully it won't be awful." Miranda didn't want the noise to drive her assistant crazy, but she was so anxious to get going. She wondered if that was why she'd had a dreadful feeling and hoped her construction guy wasn't about to call and cancel or delay her project.

"It'll be fine," Darby said. "The Thorne family will be gone by the time the noisy construction starts and if anyone else comes in, I'll simply be forthright about the possible construction noise during the day over the next eight months in that side of the Inn."

"Excellent."

Miranda said goodbye to her friend and employee and headed to her room. She couldn't stop thinking about the weird feeling she'd had earlier, before chatting with Darby. She sort of hoped the feeling represented the surprise of the new guests and the unexpected income the Inn would get. Unfortunately, she didn't think that was it. A ten-day, four-room business boon was awesome, but likely not enough to generate the feeling she'd had. She was unconvinced good news would make her feel like her very breath had been slammed out of her lungs.

Determined not to let the odd near-premonition drag her down, she dismissed it. Whatever was coming, she'd just have to deal with it as best she could, like she always did.

If nothing else, Miranda was forewarned. She'd be on the lookout, but she refused to worry about whatever was coming.

Chapter Three

William Cole looked into the full-length mirror in the master bathroom walk-in closet and tried to gauge what others would see when once he got ready and went out into the world. He always wanted to make the best possible impression on others.

First, though, he sucked in his belly and pushed out his chest. That looked much better, in his biased estimation. He probably needed to do more sit-ups, but perhaps he'd schedule another liposuction to rid him of the flab that lingered around his midsection instead.

It was easier, more effective and, best of all, a much faster way to see guaranteed results than simple exercise could provide. Yes. That belly flab had to go. He wanted to look his best. He wanted to look as healthy as possible.

He leaned in and took a closer look at his face. The eyelid lift and the neck lift surgery he'd had done a while back had taken years off his looks. Maybe even a decade. Maybe more.

Dr. Thackery was the most talented plastic surgeon in the county, in William's opinion. At

William's final post-operative appointment after his neck lift surgery, the doctor had recommended a very in-demand nurse practitioner for William's further aftercare.

He wanted to help William keep up with the amazing plastic surgery that had been done and told him to go find Helga Bergen and see *if* he could get an appointment with her.

William had called that very day and managed to get a consultation. While Helga hadn't wanted to take on any more clients, William had managed to talk her into it with quite a bit of pleading. Once he turned on the charm, he felt he could accomplish pretty much anything he wanted. Pretty much.

These days, Helga administered his Botox injections, his fillers and all the other recommended vitamin mixtures and intravenous fluids he needed for his new healthy self-care management regimen.

Yes, it all came at a cost. However, he was worth it. After all, he was doing what he considered proactive measures to look and feel younger, which translated into what he considered a healthier lifestyle. There was absolutely nothing wrong with being more healthy.

The fairly reasonable cost was worth every penny, to his way of thinking. Unfortunately, his wife hadn't thought the cost of his self-care regime was worth the price. Miranda regularly rolled her eyes whenever he got a new procedure done these days, but he didn't appreciate her sullen attitude and she was wrong. So very wrong.

In fact, she'd been totally against his eyelid and neck surgery from the start. It had taken him a long time to convince her that he was going to do it whether she approved or not.

They had fought about it even after he'd had the surgery. That was completely foolish, to his way of thinking. He'd already had it done. He couldn't take it back even if he wanted to, and he most certainly didn't. She needed to just get used to it and stop complaining.

To that end, he hadn't whispered a word to Miranda about his completely necessary aftercare with Helga, either. She wouldn't understand it or want to spend the money on it.

Therefore, he'd gotten a credit card in his name only to use, so he wouldn't have to argue with Miranda about his health needs on a regular basis. Arguing about needed care wasn't healthy at all, and he refused to participate.

He also hadn't mentioned to his wife that he'd cut his hours from a four-day, full-time arrangement to what was called extended part-time. He'd tried to talk to Miranda about doing it last year and a person would have thought he suggested pulling the food right out of their children's mouths if he reduced his workload by even an hour.

Miranda behaved as though it didn't matter that their children were all grown and gone from their home. Good thing she didn't know he made the move in his hours soon after bringing it up with her.

She griped and moaned about their medical insurance, but since it wasn't paying for any of his healthy lifestyle choices, he didn't think they needed it anymore. And what she didn't know wouldn't cause any more arguments between them. He refused to feel guilty about it.

William also decided he didn't feel guilty about keeping his aftercare from his wife, not at all. She didn't need to know about anything she would only pick a fight with him over. He was tired of the constant battles and arguments over the way he wanted to live his life.

To that end, he pondered again, and not for the first time, that maybe they'd been together long enough. Maybe it was past time for something new and more exciting for the rest of his years. That notion was starting to take root in his mind and grew appreciably stronger every day.

Then again, his reduced salary after going part-time behind Miranda's back barely covered his treatments. His employer offered the barest medical insurance for him and his spouse while he worked a four-day, full-time schedule, but the reduction in his workload to extended part-time meant he didn't qualify for even limited benefits.

Miranda would have gone ballistic much sooner if she'd known they only had the barest of medical coverage last year. Luckily, they hadn't needed it, so William felt justified in letting it go.

Her only concern regarding his job was the stupid medical insurance that considered his life-style changes for bettering his health optional, or rather elective, to use *their* stupid terminology. So since it was not available for his needs, it had been an easy decision to do without it.

These days, William went to work every day in the morning like he had before, but he then took extended an extended lunch and only worked a couple of hours in the afternoons.

Miranda was none the wiser and that suited him just fine. She didn't need to know about his shorter work hours or his salary cut and espe-cially not that he'd gone to extended part-time sta-tus, thereby removing the medical insurance they clearly didn't need anyway.

It would just cause another argument and nothing was going to change regardless of her feel-ings. He didn't want to work longer at the bank. He had other irons in the fire, so to speak. Miranda had never known about his few and far between *side* jobs.

Unfortunately, his salary had been cut by al-most sixty percent. It meant he'd had to do many more side jobs to supplement his income for his new healthy lifestyle.

It was a good thing Miranda had made such a success out of her little B&B business. And the reason he hadn't done anything to jeopardize his marriage. Admittedly, he needed Miranda, at least for now.

Sometime in the near future, he was going to need to pull some money out of their joint savings account and open one in his name only. Just like he had done with his new secret credit card.

He'd even had to procure a P.O. Box in town to send the credit card bills there, in order to keep it from Miranda. If she found out about his secret credit card or his secret P.O. Box, she'd flip out, lecture him and then there would be more arguing.

No, thank you very much. That simply wouldn't do.

The biggest objection he had was the price he paid to keep his one credit card bill away from his wife. Then again, he had his treatment receipts sent there, as well. Soon, he was going to have to get another credit card to supplement the first for his aftercare and future very necessary surgeries. Then maybe the expense of keeping his secret credit cards from Miranda would be worth the price.

Maintaining a clandestine life could be expensive, but he secretly enjoyed the thrill. It was exciting. Every time he visited his P.O. Box to retrieve his mail, William felt like a secret agent receiving classified documents for an important mission.

Still, even with a second credit card, or a third one, William needed more money. He pondered what would be a fair amount to take from their joint savings account. Miranda would say half or maybe even none, given her poor attitude of late, but he'd worked during their marriage, too. He was willing to admit that he'd contributed absolutely nothing in the last several years, but they were married. She owed him.

Miranda had been saving up to build an extension for her Driftwood Inn, but he felt the part of the marriage vows that talked about "richer or poorer" were still appropriate. He deserved a significant portion of the savings as his due for having to put up with his wife these last several years.

She was becoming more and more shrewish as time went on, not less. One day she'd make that distasteful frown face one too many times and just turn into a small rodent, twitching, snarling and scratching all his hopes and dreams away.

It wasn't fair that he didn't have money. Miranda wasn't being fair at all.

Therefore, taking half of the balance in the savings account was probably fair. He'd think about it and decide once he was at the bank. He hoped she hadn't moved the money to her business account. That was in her name only on purpose.

He'd insisted on it long ago, in case her business failed. He'd expected her to last maybe two years, five if she got lucky, and then be forced to close down, having failed miserably. Shockingly, she had succeeded. And that had been good for him for a few years.

William wasn't listed on the business account except in the event of Miranda passing away. Even then he only got twenty percent, as the other eighty went to their grown children. Like they should get such a big chunk of Miranda's business when William needed the money more than they did.

Because, unfortunately, his credit card was almost at maximum capacity. He'd only been making the minimum payments in order to purchase new clothing that wasn't as stodgy as what he used to wear. He couldn't look as youthful as he did and walk around in old man's clothes, could he? No. He could not.

And he'd already called and tried to increase his limit, but had been turned down. That also was completely unfair, but he couldn't do anything about it right now. The credit card company had wanted another income listed on his account before approving an increase in his credit limit, but he couldn't send them Miranda's income as a secondary card holder. If he did, she'd find out about the secret credit card.

He spent quite some time pondering different ways to get some money to keep living the lifestyle he'd become accustomed to. That was his primary goal. He would try to get a new credit card and then pay the minimum amount on that, too, if he could. If that didn't work, he'd have to see about drumming up some side jobs to supplement his dwindling income.

Miranda had rolled her eyes when she saw

the new suit he'd purchased at a hip clothing store for admittedly a slightly younger clientele last week. She told him he looked ridiculous.

Well, she didn't use the actual word *ridiculous*, but the rolling of her eyes certainly told him how she felt. William decided quickly that it was *her* problem, not his. If she couldn't see the benefits of this new healthy lifestyle, then he felt sorry for her. She certainly wasn't a spring chicken any longer. Maybe if she wasn't so against looking younger, they could have a future together.

Alas, Miranda was firmly planted in the *anti*-looking younger camp. William was pro doing anything to look younger, which to him translated into looking healthier. And if looking healthier also made him look younger, then so be it.

The Botox treatments had been amazing for his aftercare. In fact, William had another appointment this afternoon with Helga and Kaylee, her young medical assistant.

Kaylee was a very sweet girl. At the tender age of twenty-one, she seemed much older than her years. She was smart and had what he considered very sound ideas about life and how it should be lived to the fullest. He adored her zest for fun and just being in her presence made him feel twenty years younger. Maybe more.

William bent his head down, noticing—and not for the first time—that his hair was getting to be more salt than pepper. He'd have to do something about that and soon. It wouldn't do to have a forty-year-old face and a sixty-year-old hair color.

William made a mental note to stop by his barber today, before heading to work, and have a serious chat about his options to take out the bulk —or maybe even all—of the salt and only leave the pepper in his hair.

Then he would truly look like a decade and a half had been removed from his overall appearance. Maybe even two decades. That would be amazing. Looking younger always made him *feel* younger, too.

He glanced over his shoulder at his wife, Miranda, still in bed asleep, and realized that he looked much younger than she did, even though he was four years older than her. He'd tried to get her interested in doing something to make herself look younger, but she'd only gotten angry about it.

Whatever.

If she didn't want to improve herself and look younger, he couldn't make her. That was in his mind the more *ridiculous* eye-rolling attitude.

William turned back to the mirror and ran his fingers across his forehead, where he'd recently had a Botox treatment, and marveled at how the wrinkles had disappeared like magic.

Kaylee, who helped monitor all of his treatments, was perhaps the sweetest girl he'd ever met. She was also the most enthusiastic fan about how he looked, complimenting him repeatedly on the improving progress of his appearance with each injection and intravenous dose of special vitamins that were administered each week.

Miranda would have a cow—maybe several —if she found out how much he was spending, but every day William was finding it easier to care *less* about what she thought.

His wife's entire life was basically stagnating in the front lobby of the Driftwood Inn. She only lived, breathed and cared about her precious B&B.

And while he was willing to admit that her business had helped them out of financial trouble a time or two over the past few years, he still wouldn't have put in the massive amount of energy and effort that she did in order to make a living.

His thoughts for his future seemed to be aligned more with Kaylee's way than Miranda's. It was unfortunate, but likely warranted. He was practically a whole new person and his wife refused to even consider getting even a little bit healthy, like he was. It was, therefore, her loss and he shouldn't be dragged down by her foolish ideas of how the next part of his new life should be lived.

William was growing more and more interested in Kaylee as more than a good friend. She had called him William from the start, even when he told her she could call him Bill like everyone else did.

Kaylee told him she preferred the name William, as it sounded very dignified and then gave him a dazzling smile. From that point on, he'd been introducing himself as William instead of Bill. It *did* make him feel more distinguished. More important. Yes. He liked that feeling quite a lot. And it had been because of Kaylee. He was very appreciative of her understanding and continual encouragement as he went through his transformation into a younger-looking, more healthy person.

William had only known Kaylee for a few months, but felt like they had built up a great and very close friendship in that short time. He wondered regularly if she would be interested in going out for a nice friendly lunch. Perhaps he could take her somewhere she wouldn't normally be able to afford.

They could chat about his progress on his personal improvement and what she thought about his efforts. He could ask her about her career and future and maybe even recommend something to help her with her goals. That would be very nice of him. And given how much she'd done to boost his self-confidence, he practically owed it to her to return the favor.

William didn't care if anyone saw them together, either. He wasn't do anything wrong. He was merely appreciating a young woman who had been very good to him and offering her a very small reward for her kindness and help as he pursued his new healthy lifestyle.

He hadn't asked as of yet, because he didn't want to scare her off. But the more time that went by, the more he felt like Kaylee maybe *wanted* him to ask her to a nice lunch.

So, after he visited his barber, stopped by work to get a few things done in order not to be fired, he would go get his treatment before lunch and chat with her as usual. Then, when the time was right, William planned to ask her out for a nice, totally innocent and friendly lunch.

In truth, it was exciting just to think about it. He hoped she would accept. And why wouldn't she? It was totally innocent. Wasn't it?

That would be his sign. If she accepted his invitation to lunch, then that meant he was on the right track for his future. If she refused, perhaps he'd readjust his thinking. Perhaps.

Surely she'd accept. *Of course she'd want to go out for a friendly lunch,* he reassured himself.

William then had a very nice time imagining what it would be like to not only live with but also be with a much younger woman. His daydream was so satisfying and good, William suddenly had a new goal in mind for his future.

The daydream of being with Kaylee perked him up faster than any of his much-needed surgeries ever had.

William decided that it must be fate that he and Kaylee had met at a point where he needed to change his stagnant life into a better healthier lifestyle.

He chose to allow fate to determine his future and didn't plan to look in the rearview mirror.

Chapter Four

Miranda listened as her husband primped in front of the mirror of their shared walk-in closet. She tried to fall back asleep, though it was a wasted effort. He managed to make quite a lot of noise, mumbling to himself and banging into walls and doors as he got ready for work.

It was as if he thought he lived alone. Well, he didn't.

Bill also didn't bother to keep the lights off or even on a low setting to be the tiniest bit considerate. It was as though she didn't live here or require any sleep. She also worked very hard in her career, but it didn't make her husband considerate.

Clearly, her need for sleep didn't matter to him. She knew it to be true. She'd talked to him about it before. More than once. By the end of the heated argument that resulted each and every time she brought it up, somehow her lack of sleep turned out to be her own fault and not that *he* was waking her up every morning by being inconsiderate and making so much noise.

Lately, their arguments were *always* her

fault, at least according to Bill. Miranda would have gotten up and said something today as well, but it would have started yet another disagreement and she wasn't in the mood to start her day that way. Not anymore.

Clearly he wasn't going to change back to the civil man he'd once been. Since all the arguments were her fault, picking a fight with him wouldn't change a single thing. Better to just seethe in silence. Perhaps she'd get some ear plugs to block out his loud morning preparations to greet the day. At least that way she might get some sleep or at least avoid more verbal sparring.

In fact, she was pretty tired of every conversation they had lately turning into a quarrel. She closed her eyes and pretended she couldn't hear all the noise he made, shoving her hands over her hears, even though it generally didn't help much. She made another mental note to get ear plugs, knowing she'd likely forget again.

She sighed and rolled over, turning her back on him, with a vow to *try* and get some more sleep, even though it was like trying to sleep while a wild animal bashed its way through a shop full of glass.

It was interesting to her that while this unpleasantness between them had been growing for some time, it was as if she woke up one day and it was suddenly a big, huge problem.

Bill hadn't been acting like himself for quite a few years, but she was too busy with the Inn to stop and cater to what she considered his unreasonable whims.

He'd already spent thousands of dollars on completely unnecessary plastic surgery to tuck away and smooth out the interesting lines on his face, especially the ones around his eyes.

Once upon a time, Miranda had loved Bill's eyes and the character lines that formed when he smiled. But she didn't love his eyes anymore because the character lines had been completely erased. Now his eyes looked plastic and phony. No lines whatsoever were visible. It was like he'd been puttied, smoothed and baked to a fine, fake finish.

Every time she looked at him, she was reminded of the months upon months of battles she'd fought with him regarding his desire to perk up his look so he could feel better about himself. He considered this all part of pursuing a healthy lifestyle. Miranda did not think any of this was healthy, but telling him that only made them argue more.

Miranda didn't want him to feel bad about himself. And it wasn't completely about the money, but plastic surgery seemed so invasive, so permanent and well, so…unnecessary.

She'd lost the eyelids surgery battle first. She'd lost the neck lift surgery battle soon after that. She only found out about the liposuction surgery the day before he went into the doctor's office to get the procedure.

He didn't even tell her about the second round of liposuction until after it was done and he needed a ride home to recuperate. That had been a very uncomfortable, silent and stilted drive to the house. Not much conversation had been exchanged and he never said he was sorry for springing it on her.

What bothered her the most was that the day before his second liposuction surgery, she'd specifically asked him where he'd be, because she had an important meeting with Theo Jackson to go over the final blueprints and construction plans for the expansion at the Driftwood Inn. Bill had shrugged like he had nothing out of the ordinary going on the next day. As far as Miranda was concerned, he lied to her face.

When his ride fell through after his surgery, he called her in the middle of her meeting and demanded a ride home. "Right now, Miranda." When she'd protested, he said, "No. I can't wait until the end of your *meeting*. I'm in pain." As if she were the one who'd forgotten to pick him up after his clandestine surgery. Well, she wasn't. She was the injured party who was always made to feel like *she* was the big problem. She wasn't *any* part of this problem.

On top of that, given that every month he was unable to move one part of his face, Miranda was fairly certain he was getting Botox treatments to continue to make himself *feel better* on the sly.

If he hadn't become so egotistical and single-minded about his appearance, she would have been concerned about his mental health. The few times she'd tried to suggest counselling as a way to figure out why he felt he need to change the way he looked, he had become offended and verbally attacked her. He said that maybe she was the one who needed counselling to figure out why she had to constantly undermine his attempts at self-improvement.

She'd finally given up when she realized that he really didn't see anything wrong with what he was doing. It wasn't like he was the only man out there trying to chase down his fading youth. She'd tried to be understanding, accommodating. She'd tried cajoling, then arguing. Nothing worked. Bill was going to do what Bill wanted to do. Looking back on their marriage, she wondered if part of him had always been like that, and she'd overlooked it for the sake of family harmony. Without the kids at home, with only her and Bill together, perhaps she could no longer overlook it and Bill, in turn, gave free reign to his self-centeredness.

Regardless, it was getting more difficult by the day to ignore the cracks in their marriage. They had become virtual strangers, with totally different lives and dreams.

And so, Bill never told her anything about his treatments. But what did he think? That after being married to him for all these years she wasn't supposed to notice all the lies he was telling her right to her face?

Well, she did notice and it...well, it hurt. She hated being lied to more than anything else in the world. The Bill she married used to know that. Apparently the Botox had made him forget about caring for her feelings along with their nearly thirty years of marriage. He'd changed so much, Miranda barely recognized him anymore.

He was also somehow covertly paying for these treatments, because the bills weren't showing up on any of their joint accounts or credit cards. She should be happy about it, but she wasn't. It was deceptive. He'd never been that way early in their marriage, at least to the best of her knowledge.

Bill's secrecy about all of this supposed self-improvement made her even angrier the more she thought about it. He had turned into a sneaky, shifty man she couldn't trust. He never confided anything in her anymore and he rolled his eyes and got grumpy every time she mentioned anything about the Driftwood Inn. Or his new plastic look. Or his job. Or pretty much any topic that was brought up.

Miranda spent at least a few minutes each and every day admitting to herself that she needed to have a big conversation with him about their lives, their future together. It was long overdue. But she always found a way to justify putting it off.

Then again, if she asked for a sit-down to talk to him about their future, he'd probably say he was too busy primping in every single mirror or reflective surface that he came across to ensure he looked as young as possible. And *that* was his future.

He'd suggested a time or two that she might want to get some work done on her face. She had been so insulted she hadn't been able to speak to him civilly for days. The notion she needed to *get some work done* still hurt her way deep down.

After she declined to get any plastic surgery done, he kept at it, asking when she was going to choose a healthy lifestyle. His callous persistence made her feel ugly and old.

While he hadn't used those words, she could tell that every one of the few times he actually looked at her in the face, he was assessing what she *could* look like if only she'd understand his new found love of plastic surgery and apply some to herself.

Well, he'd be waiting a very long time. She liked her face. She didn't want to look any different. She'd worked hard for the wrinkles and loved her laugh lines. Bill used to like them, too. She missed the man she'd married and spent almost all of her adult life with.

Miranda wanted to know where *her* Bill was. Where was the old Bill? The one she'd wanted to grow old with? The father of her children who was her partner in crime and friend and confidant.

Apparently, that Bill had been possessed by some sort of conceited, unprincipled fiend who only worried about looking younger than everyone around him and considered that the most important thing in life. Well, Miranda disagreed.

He looked like a foolish old goat, trying to hold on to a youthful appearance that was never, ever going to look natural. She would pity anyone else she saw acting his way, but her husband's behavior simply irritated her.

To that end, every morning started for Miranda like this. Each and every single blessed morning started with Mr. Primp, Bang and Mumble, keeping her awake before she needed to be up and about.

Was it too much to ask to just not be so rude? If they were going to live as roommates from now on, the least he could do was not ruin her sleep every single night.

After several more loud noises from the walk-in closet and then the bathroom, Miranda decided she wasn't going to be able to fall back asleep for yet another morning.

She pondered a few scenarios where she told Bill—or rather *William,* as he now preferred to be called—to get out and take his plastic, fake face with him. What would he say to that? Would he do a cheer, leap into the air and then merely leave cartoon puffs of smoke in his wake as he sprinted joyfully out of their marriage to greener, younger or maybe more plastic pastures?

Was that really what she wanted? To see him leave? Well, no. It wasn't.

She wanted things to go back to the way they'd been around their twenty-year anniversary mark. They'd been happy. They'd been a team. But those days were long gone, apparently, never to come back or even make an appearance.

Miranda tried to remember when the biggest shift in his personality had started and narrowed it down to his thirty-fifth-year class reunion, about six years back. There had been a few rifts before that, but the big change in his personality and his zeal for plastic surgery had started during that trip back to his childhood home and his high school reunion.

They'd flown to Ohio, where his parents lived until they'd passed on. They took a tour around town of the places where he'd spent time in his youth—the ice cream shop, his elementary school, the old house where he'd grown up, and a few others. They'd run into several people who told Bill he was the spitting image of his father.

Miranda thought it was sweet, but Bill had not liked the comparison.

He liked it even less when he heard it repeated again and again throughout their short trip. His father had been a notorious drunk and a mean one at that. She understood why Bill didn't want to be compared to the man, but when she tried to broach the subject, he refused talk about it, asking her not to mention it ever again. "I mean it, Miranda. I do not wish to discuss it," he'd said rather harshly to end the conversation.

At the time, Miranda had respected him enough to simply let it go. Now, she wondered if perhaps she should have tried harder to press the issue back then. Of course, she didn't know about all the changes they would face as a couple. His current transformation took several years to achieve, and it was sometimes hard to believe she'd been so complacent about it.

The reunion committee had everyone put down their email addresses when they signed in to get their reunion packet.

"Then we can all *keep in touch* going forward," the organizer had said with a big smile.

Bill had added his name and email address to the list, but mumbled that he probably wouldn't want to *go forward* with any of these people.

When Miranda considered it, she decided that while the reunion had been about the same time his attitude about his age and life had changed, he'd been withdrawing from her even before then. As she considered the timeline, she thought he'd probably started his decline when he turned fifty.

She remembered hoping that the trip to Ohio and his class reunion would cheer him up. It had not. If anything, it made his attitude worse. And from her perspective, leaving the Driftwood Inn for the weekend trip had been arduous and very stressful. She was willing to admit that her concern for her husband's mood had gone by the wayside as she focused more on her business.

Miranda knew the Inn was in good hands —her best friend in the world, Roberta, and Roberta's husband, Charlie had taken over while she and Bill were away. Their four kids had helped out of course, but it had been a very big ask when they already had the Lighthouse Inn down in Cape Canaveral Beach to run.

There hadn't been any problems or issues while she'd been gone, but Miranda knew running one B&B was quite a lot of responsibility. Taking care of two inns, even for only a long weekend, had to have been taxing.

Roberta told Miranda before she left it wasn't a problem, and reassured her of the same after she returned. She said all of the Cole children had been outstanding help, but Miranda knew it was a big workload, even with possibly begrudging and probably limited cooperation from her kids.

And, unfortunately, it hadn't really been worth it. The trip to Ohio had *not* cheered Bill up. He seemed to go downhill even faster from there. That was when he started his love affair with the mirror in their walk-in closet, taking long bouts of time to stare at himself. He would change clothes three times before making a final decision on what to wear for the day.

Miranda knew this because she was the one left to clean up the clutter of discarded clothing all over the floor of the closet. But if she brought it up, she was a shrew, a witch, a horrible person for not understanding him and what he was going through.

Soon after that, he began talking about nips and tucks and Botox and the like. Miranda hadn't taken him seriously. Perhaps she should have, though it was probably a lost cause by then. By the time he was talking about nips and tucks, he'd already made an appointment and had a surgery date scheduled before he mentioned it to her in passing, almost like he'd scheduled routine maintenance on his car.

Maybe if she'd been more proactive, it could have saved her marriage. Or maybe nothing she had done would have changed anything.

She was very unhappy. She suspected Bill was just as miserable and she didn't see any path *going forward* where the two of them remained together.

And that was a shame. It was difficult for her to throw away so many years of marriage, even though the man she married was gone. And he most assuredly didn't want to come back to her. She was tired of being the only one trying to keep their relationship going, by basically ignoring all the problems in their marriage and his attitude.

Miranda decided it was past time that she talked to a lawyer. She needed to discover what exactly would happen to the Driftwood Inn, her business and the expansion if she and Bill—or rather *William*—divorced.

Chapter Five

Nathan Cole stepped out of his truck and headed for Theo Jackson's construction office trailer. He needed to adjust his hours at his primary workplace so he could accommodate his secondary passion. The woodworking he was doing on the side in his spare time was starting to dominate his free time. He loved to craft things with wood.

Whenever he did menial repetitive tasks such as hammering nails or the like, he would let his brain work on designs he wanted to create with the various pieces of wood he'd collected. Driftwood was plentiful along the coast and what he had the most of, but he had gotten his hands on some other choice pieces of wood from various places. It was his luck they were free, otherwise he wouldn't have been able to afford them.

The storage space in the apartment he shared with his twin brother was crammed full of pieces of wood he intended to use in one project or another. He was lucky Gabe didn't complain about it. In fact, his brother, both of his sisters and is mom were very supportive of his side job. He'd even been offered a workshop at no cost where he could use some heavy woodworking equipment during the dinner hour at the local college between classes. To take advantage of it, he'd need to leave his job with Theo early.

Once they started construction on the Driftwood Inn for his mom, it was possible he'd have more flexible hours to take advantage of the free woodworking equipment. He truly wanted to make this work. He could make his rocking chairs and dining tables much faster in the more professional space at the college.

Nathan whistled as he opened the door and entered the construction office trailer at Theo Jackson's business. As expected, he immediately saw Lucy Young, Theo's receptionist, assistant and all-around right hand seated at her desk.

Lucy, as she always did, looked startled when he walked in. She dropped a pen the moment he stepped into the trailer and watched him with what appeared to be a nervous expression.

He didn't know what *that* was about, but he needed to talk to Theo about shifting his schedule so he could take advantage of the free woodworking equipment. He was a little worried that while Theo might want to help him, he might not be able to because of the commitments he'd made.

Still, there was no harm in asking. The worst he could say was, "Sorry, no can do." And Nathan would suck it up and simply spend less time on his side job. He could work at the college for half the time if Theo couldn't change his hours.

"Is Theo around?" Nathan asked, hoping his boss was close by or in his office.

Lucy brightened, as if happy to have an answer for him. "He's on his way in. Should be here in a few minutes."

Nathan nodded and gave her a smile. She swallowed hard and gestured to the row of three folding chairs along the wall next to her desk. "Would you like to wait?"

Nathan looked over his shoulder at the door and outside, where there was no one and nothing going on, and then back at the chairs. It was cooler in here than outside. So, what the heck. "Sure. I'll wait a minute or two. Thanks."

Lucy looked surprised, but a pleasant smile shaped her mouth. Nathan thought she was very pretty, but he'd heard from one of the other guys on the site that she had been either engaged to some rich dude or had a serious long-term rich boyfriend. The operable word being *rich* in both instances. If she was interested in rich, he wasn't it.

Besides, Nathan didn't mess around with women who were spoken for, no matter how many smiles and interest they sent his way. And even if she wasn't engaged or dating anyone, he was never going to be rich.

Nathan liked what he did and was looking for a woman who wanted to be more of a partner in life, not someone who was seeking a rich, status-filled life. His ideal relationship meant the two of them working together for what they achieved. He had no interest in someone looking for a sugar daddy or a credit card with benefits.

Lucy cleared her throat and said, "Our next big job is the Driftwood Inn."

Nathan nodded. "Yep. We start next week." *You're such a dolt. She knows you start next week. She likely scheduled it all.*

Thankfully, she didn't comment on his foolish remark, saying only, "That will be interesting for you, won't it? You'll be working on the place you used to live in as a kid."

Nathan shrugged. "The truth is, our family didn't actually live at the Driftwood Inn when we were growing up."

"You didn't?" Lucy's brow quirked and a dimple formed in her cheek when a sweet half-smile formed. Wow. She was *really* cute. "Where did you live?"

"There's a caretaker's cottage along the southeast side of the property next to the parking lot. It's sort of hidden behind some tall palms and other foliage. Lots of folks thought it was a garage, but it was where our family lived and where I grew up."

"Wow. I didn't know that." Her sudden grin lit up the room.

"Well, now you have some inside information."

She giggled. "I wasn't trying to get inside information, you know. I was just making conversation."

"Sure. I know. I'm just kidding." Nathan stared at her. She was *really* very pretty. Too bad she wanted a different kind of man than he'd ever be.

"Where did *you* grow up?" he asked, before he knew the words were going to come out of his mouth. He shouldn't encourage the conversation, but hated to be in a place where awkward silence was present.

Lucy's cheeks turned pink and she stammered before answering, "I'm originally from a place called Prescott, Arizona. It's a small town, you probably haven't heard of it. No one ever seems to know it."

"I can't say I've heard of Prescott, but I do like Arizona. I'll bet it's great to live there."

She nodded and continued. "Anyway, I came out to Florida when my grandparents got older and needed help. I just ended up staying here. Arizona is nice and I liked living there. My favorite was seeing mountains, but it is also very dry. I like the nice weather here where it rains on occasion and I love being so close to the ocean."

Now it was Nathan's turn to be surprised. "Oh? How long ago did you move out here?"

She looked up at the ceiling as if doing a calculation in her head. "Seven years. Wow. I hadn't counted it up in a while."

Nathan did his own calculation. If she came out here when she was eighteen, she'd be twenty-five. As he was only twenty-four, she was an older woman, though she looked like a teenager. He'd heard several people comment on how Theo's receptionist looked like a child. Theo assured everyone she was old enough to work for him, but didn't reveal her true age. No gentleman would. And neither did Theo.

Before he could ask, she said, "I was only fifteen and still in high school, but Grammy and Pops really needed some help." She shrugged as if fifteen-year-olds did that kind of thing every single day.

Nathan's mouth opened again and he asked, "You're only twenty-two?" He didn't mean to sound so shocked, but somehow twenty-two seemed vastly younger than twenty-five. It was only three years, but her admission had taken him aback.

Lucy nodded and the blush came to her cheeks once more. "I'll be twenty-three in a few months."

He nodded, definitely reassessing his opinion of Lucy Young. A girl who came to take care of her Grammy and Pops didn't seem like the kind of girl who would only be looking for a credit card with benefits. He'd have to stop listening to gossip and find out his own information from now on.

Nathan would have been happy to keep talking with Lucy, but Theo came through the door in the next moment and sidetracked his new quest for more information on someone he'd considered not his type. At least until now. Perhaps he'd take a second look.

"Hey, Nathan. What's up?"

Nathan stood up and turned from Lucy's desk to face the older man. "I just had a quick question for you about the work schedule coming up, if you have time."

"Sure thing," Theo said. He glanced at his assistant. "Any important messages, Lucy?"

"Nothing big. I left a few notes on your desk, but they aren't urgent."

"Thanks."

Nathan smiled at her as he passed by her desk on the way to Theo's office down the hall. She smiled back and he noticed pink flush her cheeks. What was that about?

And what sort of girl came all the way across the country to care for her elderly grandparents? Certainly not any women that Nathan knew. He was very intrigued by Lucy Young all of a sudden. He had enjoyed talking to her and now wanted to learn all about her.

Nathan vowed to himself that he would learn more about Lucy instead of making snap judgments based on hearsay from a bunch of grubby construction workers.

Chapter Six

Miranda was startled out of a dead sleep again the very next morning, when Bill started making even more noise than usual in the closet. Her first thought was that they were being robbed, but then she heard Bill say something about the closet not being big enough. However, it wasn't a murmur, it was a full-throated statement and it woke her even more. Sometimes she merely heard him rambling around the house and just rolled over and went back to sleep as best she could. This morning, not so much.

Bang. "This closet is far too small," Bill said, practically shouting, followed by a bad word. In the next moment, her overburdened camel crumpled completely under the weight of one too many pieces of very loud straw.

Miranda sat up in bed, fully awake and not happy about it.

Perhaps it was because she was tired. Perhaps it was because she hadn't had any caffeine yet. Perhaps she just wanted her loud husband to settle down so she could get some more sleep, but it was time to have that talk with him about courtesy yet again.

Miranda stumbled out of bed and headed to their apparently too small closet that now spurred him to spit out expletives. Loud ones.

He turned around to see her framed in the doorway, arms crossed and what was certainly a grim expression on her face. She wanted to look fearsome. She wanted him to understand she was serious. Though she did her best to look formidable, he either didn't notice or, more likely, he didn't care.

It looked like he tried to get his brows to furrow, but they didn't move. They'd been Botoxed into submission, giving him more of a squinty-eyed look whenever he tried to make any part of his face move. "What on Earth are you doing up, Miranda?"

"I'm up because you are being too loud in the closet getting ready. And since lately it happens every single day, I thought I'd make my annoyance clear to you," she said in a clearly angry tone. "Why don't you pretend that I'm trying to get some much needed sleep and be quiet for a change?"

He scoffed and shook his head as though she was accusing him unfairly. "I don't know what you are talking about Miranda."

"Don't you? Well, let me explain." She did a verbatim recitation of what she'd heard this very morning in the closet that woke her from a sound sleep. Miranda then recapped yesterday's loud closet performance and then the day before that.

By the time she finished, she was shouting.

"What do I have to do to get you to be considerate and not make so much noise in the morning?" she asked. "Do you see the dark circles under my eyes? Well, I need more sleep."

His eyes scanned her up and down. Then he shrugged and moved forward like he was going to pass by her and leave the closet. He stopped two feet from her.

"If you have dark circles, Miranda, then you should get your eyes done. I've been telling you that for some time. If you don't listen, I can't help you." He looked over one of her shoulders and into their bedroom, as if she should just take that insult and absorb it. Well, she wasn't in the mood.

"I don't need any plastic surgery, I need some sleep! You are the one keeping me awake. Stop it. What do I have to do or say to get you to be quiet in the mornings?"

His response was to sigh loudly and stare at the wall of shoe shelves. Miranda didn't budge from her place in the closet doorway. She didn't care if he was annoyed. He was going to have to stampede past her to get out before they had a chat.

Miranda took a deep breath. "We need to have a serious talk, Bill."

Bill pushed out a long, angry sigh. "William! I want to be called William," he said in a sullen tone any two-year-old would be proud to claim and use in a tantrum.

Miranda rolled her eyes. "Okay then, *William*. We need to have a serious talk. For starters, why do I need to change what I call you after nearly thirty years of marriage?"

His body straightened and she sensed he was about to launch into some long explanation about how a name was important and identified how he viewed himself in the world, yadda, yadda, yadda.

Bill opened his mouth, but Miranda spoke first. "No. Never mind. Do you agree we need to have a talk or not?"

His eyes squinted again. She wasn't sure what it meant. That squinty-eyed move had to cover a whole host of responses to questions, since it was the only part of his face he could actually move. "What do you want to talk about?" he finally asked, as if put out by the question.

"I want to talk about our future."

"Our future?" He managed to sound like he couldn't imagine their future and also made fun of the notion of it at the same time, as if it should be clear they didn't have one.

"Yes, William. Our future. Where do you see yourself in five years? And more importantly, am I there in your future?"

He just stared at her. His eyes didn't even move. After several taut, silent seconds, he glanced at his watch and was suddenly animated. "Now look at the time. Move out of my way, Miranda. I'm late. I need to go."

"Answer my questions first." *Please, Bill,*

come back from Plastic Land and talk to me.

"I don't have time. And even if I did, I don't want to." He put a palm on her shoulder and pushed past her, right out of the closet and out of their bedroom at the fastest clip she'd seen him move in a long while. Before long, she heard him banging around in the kitchen downstairs, making something to eat.

He usually just ate a bowl of cereal, so she wasn't certain why he needed to bang a pot or skillet on the stove grates, but that was what it sounded like he was doing. Again. Like he'd been doing most mornings lately. Anything to make as much noise as possible and disturb her sleep. She rolled her eyes and told herself there was no point in following him down into the kitchen because they would only argue.

Miranda shook her head, held back a grunt that might turn into a primal scream if she really let loose, and climbed back into bed. She didn't need to get up for another hour. If Bill—or rather William—wasn't going to make an effort to talk to her or answer a simple question about their future together, then maybe she already had her answer.

Were they going to continue living like roommates who didn't even get along? How long was she going to put up with that? Not long.

Miranda spent the bulk of her morning doing errands away from the Driftwood Inn, after not getting nearly enough sleep the night before. Really, it had become the norm. Even confronting her husband yesterday morning had yielded nothing. He was up at the butt crack of dawn this morning, slamming things around in the closet, the bathroom and the kitchen for an hour. An hour!

Not wanting to start another argument, Miranda simply drank an extra cup of coffee before starting her long day.

First, she went to the bank to shift some funds around and also to get a cashier's check for the first installment payment to Theo. The construction project for her addition would be starting next week. She couldn't wait until they broke ground.

Darby had volunteered to take charge of all the before, during and after photographs, for which Miranda was grateful. She wanted to document the work, but had never been good at remembering to take pictures. Bill had always done that through the years when their kids were little. Now he barely acknowledged that he had any children, let alone the desire to take photographs of them.

The person she needed to talk to at the bank regarding the status of her accounts and or changing them was unavailable for the rest of the day, so Miranda left her number to make an appointment. The receptionist promised to call and schedule one when the bank officer had an open slot.

She visited several suppliers, went to the post office, stopped at the kitchen supply store to get a few needed items for the Inn and also stopped at a new lawyer's office to set up an appointment and get things started. She was surprised that she was able to meet the lawyer for a few minutes between appointments.

She even was able to tell the lawyer briefly what she wanted talk about and get a sense of her as a person. Miranda liked her from the moment they shook hands. She set up an appointment for the next week, sooner than she'd thought she would be able to get in, and took her new lawyer's card. The lawyer told her to feel free to call her if anything changed before their scheduled appointment.

Miranda continued checking off the rest of her list of errands. Next up was filling her gas tank at the self-service pump. Soon after that chore was completed, her stomach growled. She'd been upset this morning for a number of reasons, all of them starting with the word "Bill". While she'd had that extra cup of coffee, she hadn't had much to eat. All right, she didn't have anything to eat. Did cream in her coffee count? Likely not.

Her stomach growled again. This time it was almost loud enough to wake the dead. She needed some food, so drove to the grocery store and parked nearby, as it was her final chore of the day to complete, and went to get a bite to eat. It was always better to go to the grocery store with a full stomach anyway, she thought as she rationalized the expense of eating out.

Miranda strolled to a bistro on the upscale side that also had a very nice soup and salad combo lunch special at a great price. She ordered minestrone and the house salad with ranch dressing, eating alone at a back table.

She ate slowly, taking the time to think about her morning. She had to leave her number at the bank to make an appointment. Annoying, but what could she do? Nothing. She enjoyed meeting her new divorce lawyer, if only briefly. She got enough of a feel for the woman to like her and look forward to working with her.

Miranda hadn't gone to the lawyer she and Bill had used for years because she didn't trust him not to tattle her business to Bill. Instead, she'd called Roberta and asked if she knew of any good lawyers.

Roberta had asked, "What kind of lawyer?"

"Divorce lawyer."

"Oh, no. Miranda, I'm so sorry."

"I'm not saying that's what's going to happen for certain, but all signs point that way. Bill has changed for what I consider the worst and doesn't seem interested in changing back to the man I married and raised four children with. He also scoffs when I bring up our future, making me think he doesn't want one, at least not with me."

"Again, I'm really sorry, but my daughter,

Beth, used Monica Allendale and she was really great." She gave Miranda the address in town and her rates. Miranda thought she was very reasonably priced.

"Thanks, Roberta, I appreciate it. I didn't want to ask around because I don't want to alert Bill to my plans. Our family lawyer is a big blabbermouth and he'd probably side with Bill anyway."

Roberta laughed. "Oh, Miranda, you certainly have a good attitude. But promise me that if you need anything, you'll let me know."

"I appreciate that, Roberta, and you'll be the first person I call. But I know you're busy with Dr. Hottie, so I won't abuse the privilege."

"Very funny. Harrison and I are very happily taking things slowly."

Roberta and her husband, Charlie, had been deliriously happy until he was killed in a diving accident. A year later, Roberta and her four children had a private, family-only seaside ceremony to honor Charlie.

Soon afterward, Miranda and Roberta had met for lunch. Miranda pointed out Dr. Harrison Hunt to her when he came into the out-of-town restaurant they were eating at. And now, lo and behold, Roberta and Dr. Hottie were seeing each other. Perhaps they would have met eventually, but Miranda felt like she had played a small part in helping Roberta find a nice man.

"I'm just so glad you found someone you like, whether you take it slowly or not. I'm very happy for you, Roberta."

"Well, I'll be thinking about you, Miranda. And, please, don't hesitate to call if you need a shoulder to cry on, someone to listen or just someone to talk to about anything at all. I'm here for you, always."

"Thanks, Roberta. And also thanks for the lawyer's name."

"No problem. We need to get together and chat soon, you know."

"I know, we're definitely overdue. It's just that currently, my husband is being a pain in the butt in all ways possible, the construction on my addition starts next week and I'm so busy with day-to-day life I can barely keep my head above water as it is."

"That means you need a girls lunch even more than usual, maybe even a girls night out. But I understand you have quite a lot going on these days."

Miranda longed for a girls night out with her friend more than anything, but just didn't have the time right now. However, Roberta was good people and truly her BFF. She knew when to push and when to just listen and be a good friend.

"Tell you what," Miranda said, "once they break ground next week, I'll give you a call and we'll set something up, okay?"

"Perfect."

"Thanks, Roberta. I mean it. I don't know what I'd do without you as my friend."

"Back at you, Miranda. Hang in there."

They said their good-byes and just thinking about Roberta now made Miranda feel better. Even with all the stuff she was going through with Bill, she knew she could count on her friend to not only be silent about her possible divorce plans, but to always be there for her to talk to, go out to lunch or a girls night out. She was so lucky and so truly thankful to have such a great friend in her corner.

Chapter Seven

Zoe Cole Pierce raced downstairs to catch her new hubby, Evan, before he left for work. She'd slept in for some reason and her sweet husband of only two months hadn't woken her. He usually didn't wake her on purpose, but every time he left, he made sure to kiss her goodbye, even if she was sound asleep. Sometimes she woke up, sometimes she didn't.

She had snapped awake all of a sudden when she heard Evan down in the kitchen. She dragged herself out of bed in order to get a kiss goodbye for the day that she could remember this time.

"Hey," she said. Evan was seated at the small kitchen table they'd purchased together at Happy Home Furnishings. Clearly, she hadn't missed him after all. She came in slowly, stepping carefully as she always did before any caffeine entered her body.

Evan looked up from his phone and grinned as she crossed the room toward him. "Hey. You didn't have to get up so early."

"I know, but I needed a kiss goodbye."

"I always give you a kiss goodbye before I

leave, even when you sleep in."

She shrugged. "I know. It's true. But I wanted to remember it this time." She leaned down and kissed him. He pulled her down onto his lap and gave her an unforgettable kiss.

"Wow. I should come down to breakfast with you more often," Zoe said. She settled on his lap, resting her head on his shoulder. He wrapped his arms around her middle and kissed the top of her head.

"I love you, Zoe," Evan said, squeezing her gently. He always told her he loved her. Every single day and often more times than just once a day.

"I love you, too, Evan. I'm so happy. Two months into this marriage and I'm still giving you two thumbs way up as a husband."

"Awesome. Two months down, fifty-plus years to go. I'm on a roll."

He kissed her again. She glanced at the clock and knew he needed to leave. He hated to be late to work. And even though he owned his own business, and could set his hours to anything he wanted, Evan was adamant about being there early every day.

And that made Zoe love her husband even more. He was always dependable in everything he did.

Zoe stood up, reluctantly, knowing he had to go pretty soon. She leaned down and kissed him once more.

"What are you doing today?" he asked, as she

crossed the room to get her first cup of coffee of the day.

"I've got a class later and an appointment with my college advisor," she said absently. Professor Lambert had called yesterday and made the quick appointment for today. They did need to discuss her next semester, but Zoe thought she had plenty of time. Even so, best to get it out of the way so she'd know what her next year looked like.

"Oh, yeah?" Evan asked.

Zoe fixed her coffee the way she liked it, sweet and creamy. Took a sip and her brain functions became much clearer. "Well, since I passed flower arranging class with flying colors, I'm only a few credits and an internship away from getting my hospitality degree, at long last."

Evan, of course, knew why she hadn't gotten her college degree yet, even though she should be two years or so out of college by now. He was very supportive of her education, even at this late date.

He asked, "Are you sorry you took a couple of years off to help with your aunt?"

"Nope. I have no regrets whatsoever. Besides, she left me enough money to buy the house we live in."

Her husband looked around the room with an appreciative eye. "It's a really great house." Evan stood up from the kitchen table, took his dishes to the sink, rinsed them and put them in the dishwasher. He was a good husband and an even better roommate. She loved living with him.

"I know, this really attractive guy helped me pick it out. Wonder what happened to him?" she asked with a smile.

"I heard he got married to the love of his life and lived happily ever after," Evan said without missing a beat.

"I heard that, too. His wife is a lucky girl."

Evan closed the dishwasher door, turned and kissed her once more, wrapping her in his strong arms for a bear hug before releasing her. "See you tonight."

"Can't wait."

Zoe watched his car pull onto the quiet street they lived on and drive away as she sipped her coffee. He was a keeper, that one.

Her phone rang, jarring her from her goofy feelings of love for Evan. She didn't even look at the screen, just answered, "Hello?"

"Hi, Zoe, it's Mom. Are you coming over to the Driftwood Inn today? And if so, when? I wasn't sure what your schedule was this week."

"Hi, Mom. I'll be over later this afternoon and I'll write down my schedule then. I have a class at ten and a meeting with my college advisor at eleven today. Why? Do I need to be there sooner?"

"No, the afternoon is fine. The contractor is coming over at three o'clock to go over the final plans for the expansion. I wanted you here, too. If everything is okay with the final plans, they will break ground next week." Her mom sounded really happy.

"Awesome," Zoe said.

Her mother certainly deserved to be happy. She'd worked very hard to make the Driftwood Inn a big success over the years. The expansion was going to take seven or eight months, if everything went well and there was no bad weather or significant hurricanes in the summer months.

She had her fingers crossed that it would be a smooth renovation for the Driftwood Inn. Most every year, there were a few months where they were fully booked. With the extension added on to the north side of the original building, they'd have a two-story addition featuring six brand new bedrooms with luxury bathrooms, a new common area on the lower level and a loft with a library on the second floor with tables and chairs scattered about as another gathering area for guests or for functions.

The new addition to the Driftwood Inn was going to be beautiful.

Once the expansion was completed—hopefully by Christmas—her mother said she would be well on her way to a comfortable retirement.

Zoe considered how her mother was phrasing things lately, where she didn't say *we* anymore, but instead *me*. Lately, it didn't seem like Zoe's parents were getting along. Actually, it had been much longer than just lately. It had been years in the making.

It was also not even remotely her mother's fault. Zoe blamed her father because he had changed into a self-centered idiot, trying to look like he was in his thirties even though he'd be sixty next year.

And there was no talking to him about it, either. He was bound and determined to plastic surgery himself into looking like what he considered to be healthier. But he *didn't* look healthy. Zoe thought he looked like he'd already had too much work done on his face.

Heck, most of the times she'd seen him in the past few month, part of his face was paralyzed. And it was a different part every time she saw him. She couldn't even imagine how much it cost. It was surely quite a lot.

"It is awesome. Oh, before I forget, let me tell you what happened at the Inn yesterday." Her mother went on to tell her about the registration glitch at the Pineapple Cove Inn along with their ten-day, four-room guest acquisition. Including the part where they charged full price for their rooms and the guy was happy to pay it. Zoe wasn't all that surprised, considering the family's alternative might have been going back home to Montana without a beachside vacation.

"That's great news, Mom. Too bad about the Pineapple Cove Inn, but even the old owners were sort of snotty at times. Plus, I've heard the son was much the same way as his parents even before he took over."

"I'm just glad they found us instead of heading back to Montana."

"I know you're excited about this expansion, Mom. I think it will be wonderful to have six rooms added on to the Driftwood Inn. And I know you'll make more money with the addition." Zoe vowed to do whatever she could to help her mother with this coming renovation, because her mother had worked so hard to make the Driftwood Inn a success. She always had been a hard worker, no matter what she was working on. Even so, she usually spent most of her time thinking of others before she worried about herself.

Zoe's two younger brothers, twins Nathan and Gabe, and her older sister, Beverly, were of the same mind regarding their father and his foolish antics regarding his appearance. They all hoped it was a phase he'd grow out of or something, but after so much time along this path without any change for the better, it didn't seem likely.

Her mother said, "Thanks, Zoe. I appreciate that. And I *am* very excited about it. I'll see you this afternoon, honey."

"Okay, Mom. See you then." She hung up and went to get more coffee. She had a couple of hours before she had to be at the campus for her class. She *did* need to call Beverly and check up on her, as well.

Beverly and her husband were going through a rough patch. She'd stayed with Zoe at her new house a couple of months ago when they had a fight and she stormed out.

Zoe had to turn Evan away at the last minute

when he arrived—with a nice Italian dinner in hand—in order for Zoe to be a shoulder to cry on for her distraught sister.

It had been before they eloped, but Zoe had been so grateful that he understood and didn't get upset. He'd even given up his own dinner.

The good news was that Evan told her later he was able to accomplish something rather remarkable while they'd been apart that night. He'd mended a relationship filled with animosity and gained a good friend in the process.

Evan and Derek Covington, who ran the Cape Canaveral General Store, were business rivals of a sort for a short time because someone awful had lied and told them untrue stories about each other.

However, when Derek started secretly dating Evan's little sister, Erin, they had to make up for the sake of love. That's what Evan had told her and it still made Zoe smile.

She dialed her sister's number, but only got voicemail. She left a message and said, "Hey Beverly, it's Zoe. I'm just checking to see how you're doing. Call me later on tonight, if you want. Love you. Bye."

As she hung up the phone, Zoe remembered the last time she and Beverly had been together in downtown Cape Canaveral North. They'd run into their father, who was leaving his workplace at ten in the morning. That had been odd by itself, but the further conversation made it clear Bill Cole had not changed back into the father they'd grown up with.

He had purposely said, "Hello, Zoe. How are *you* doing?" as he'd glanced at his watch several times. Clearly, he was on his way to somewhere he considered very important, but the odd and terrible part about that day was when he ignored Beverly completely. He acted as though she wasn't standing right there with them on the street in front of his workplace. Zoe thought it had been awful.

She kept looking at Beverly and trying to get the two of them to talk, but neither Beverly nor their father seemed interested in mending the fence between them that had been broken, torn down and dragged for miles in the wake of Beverly's wedding two years before.

Their father had absolutely *not* approved of Beverly marrying Noah Peyton in any way, shape or form. It didn't matter what anyone said to him. Bill Cole was adamant that she not *involve* herself with *those people*, as he called Beverly's future in-laws and family. And he said so at every opportunity, even when he wasn't asked specifically.

Zoe didn't know what the true issue was, but it had not changed from their father's perspective in the two years that Beverly and Noah had been married.

At the time, Zoe had chalked part of her father's attitude to his defiance about wanting to change his looks with a nip here and a tuck there.

However, it had been more than that, as it turned out. And once he dug in, he was not easily motivated to change his mind about his continual improvements, as he sometimes called them.

Beverly had to beg him to walk her down the aisle. She also told him the secret of why they were *really* getting married. She was pregnant. That had also made their father angry, but he'd calmed down soon after.

It was as if marrying for love wasn't nearly a good enough reason to associate with *those people*, but an innocent child brought a different and less volatile aspect to the situation.

Their father had broken down and agreed to walk Beverly down the aisle for her wedding to Noah Peyton, even though he frowned the whole time and in every single posed wedding photo that day.

Beverly had to have the photographer touch up the group photos so he didn't look so maniacally unhappy in all her cherished keepsake wedding albums.

It wasn't completely the celebratory event it should have been. A week before the wedding, Beverly lost the baby. When she told Noah about it, he shrugged and married her anyway. No one but the two of them knew she had lost the baby before they got married.

When she found out much later, Zoe thought of Noah as being sweet, but later decided he was simply acting out against his parents because his mother especially didn't want the wedding to take place. At least Noah's parents didn't do anything to him after they found out. At least they didn't pretend he didn't exist, like Bill Cole treated his eldest daughter.

The moment their father learned she'd lost the baby *before* the wedding, he was incredibly angry. He stopped talking to Beverly the moment he found out about the miscarriage and its timing.

He acted like he only had only one daughter and Zoe knew it was hurtful for Beverly. He told everyone in the family that if he'd known beforehand, he would never have walked Beverly down the aisle. He swore he'd never forgive her for what he considered a grievous deception.

Zoe thought very highly of Noah for choosing to marry Beverly when he didn't really *have* to. But eventually he adopted the same attitude as his family regarding his and Beverly's union. From Zoe's perspective, it seemed to her as though Noah now believed wholeheartedly that Beverly and the Coles weren't really country club material. It was the gist of the big blowup he and Beverly had before she stayed with Zoe for a couple of weeks.

The Peyton family had decided that Beverly wasn't good enough for their precious son. They had probably thought that all along. She didn't have enough status as the daughter of a B&B owner. That her father worked in a bank wasn't in the same stratosphere or nearly as good as *owning* a bank, putting him in the same boat as their mother on the social scale of nice, but not meeting the high country club mark of acceptability.

Beverly and her family were too working-class. Too pedestrian. Too crass when around their friends and family and, most important of all, their country club friends. The Cole family wouldn't qualify for a membership at the club, even if they'd wanted one, and Zoe knew her parents did not want any part of the snooty country club life. Well, she didn't know how her father felt about that lately, but long ago he'd huffed and rolled his eyes at the thought of ever belonging to a snooty social club.

Zoe and Beverly's mom had begged and pleaded for them to all get along after the wedding was over, when the whole story about the pregnancy and subsequent miscarriage before the wedding was revealed.

However, Bill Cole was not going to be told how to act or what to do regarding the wedding of his eldest daughter, not even by his wife. Because, as he said regularly, "Beverly could have gotten out of that travesty of a marriage to *those people*, but she chose not to and I will not forgive her. Ever."

It had caused a terrible rift in their family. Zoe was fairly certain that her father stood alone in the matter of Beverly's wedding to Noah Peyton. All her siblings thought Noah did the honorable thing by marrying Beverly anyway.

Nathan and Gabe also thought their father was being unreasonable. Gabe had even told him that more than once, but their father was un-moved by anyone's opinion but his own in the matter. He refused to forgive Beverly no matter what anyone said to him.

It made Zoe wonder if something else was at play. Had one of Noah's family members done something to make their father into the wrath-filled man he turned out to be? She didn't know and didn't know how to find out. She put that mys-tery on the back burner for another time.

Zoe cleared her mind of any and all fam-ily issues and concentrated on her coming day. She loafed around the house, spent some time on her fabulous master bedroom deck with coffee in hand, the sun in her face, thinking about how good her life was. And tried not to feel guilty that both her mom and Beverly were not in the best of places regarding their marriages.

She hoped Beverly would work things out with Noah, but it seemed to Zoe that was likely going to be determined by Noah's very rich family. And if that was true, Beverly was likely going to be pushed out of her husband's life.

The Peytons had also been against Beverly and Noah's wedding, but they had the fortitude and class not to be public about it like Bill Cole was. Instead, they talked behind Beverly's back about her *simple* upbringing and how she couldn't pos-sibly understand the life of a wealthy person hav-ing not been raised that way. Or something to that effect, and that had been translated from Beverly's anger about it when she stayed with Zoe.

Zoe didn't blame her sister. If she got treated like that, she didn't know what she would do. Perhaps misbehave and invite their disapproval as a defense mechanism.

Chapter Eight

Beverly Cole Peyton sat in her kitchen sipping a new purple smoothie recipe she had discovered in the latest issue of *Everything at Home* magazine. It had frozen blueberries, blackberries and raspberries. She had found a mix in the frozen section at the grocery store that had all three berries in one bag. It was very convenient for many recipes. Also, it was pretty tasty to the sprinkle mixed berries over the top of a warm, steaming bowl of oatmeal.

In the smoothie recipe, there was also one ripe banana, a cup of baby spinach and half a cup of vanilla almond milk. Beverly added more almond milk because she liked to drink her smoothie with a straw and not spoon out a thicker version. Either way, it was tasty. She couldn't even see the spinach when blended with the blueberries and the banana gave it enough sweetness to make it delicious without adding any refined sugar.

Beverly waited for Noah to come down from their bedroom. She always got up way before he did, even if she stayed up late the night before. One day it might catch up with her, but not so far.

She'd always been a morning person. The minute her eyes opened, she couldn't stay in bed a second longer. She almost leapt out of bed each morning, ready to get started with the day. Meanwhile, her sister Zoe was barely awake an hour after rising, stumbling around and drinking two or more cups of coffee first thing. She smiled in memory of spending time with her sister recently, when she and Noah had been having a serious argument.

It was the reason she'd gotten up so early this morning. She wanted to be prepared to greet Noah this morning. They had some things to talk about. He might not agree, but she planned to talk to him whether he wanted to or not. It was long past due.

She'd made enough smoothie mix for him to have some, too. If he wanted to try it. More likely than not, he'd say, "No, thanks. I'm headed for the club. I'll eat there." Like he had pretty much every single day of their marriage.

He would then promptly leave the house after maybe giving her a perfunctory peck on the forehead. Or what was happening more and more was that he wouldn't even touch her at all before leaving for the entire day.

Beverly was consumed by the idea that even though he'd seemed happy when she returned after a short separation, when she'd stayed with Zoe, that wasn't the case anymore. Day by day for the last couple of months, Noah was growing more and more distant.

It had gotten to the point where they barely spoke for ten minutes a day. And that was mostly her listening to him rail or complain about his work or his frustrating day with what he called lesser people. She didn't want to know what he called them privately.

Once they were in bed, he would make a kiss noise in her direction and turn away from her, falling asleep instantly. She knew he was really asleep and not faking it, because he snored like a bear with chronic bronchitis when he slept.

In the last month especially, he left the house every morning before eight and, more often than not, didn't return until after nine at night. In the hours he *was* at home with her, he slept for eight or nine of them. That left about an hour of together time, where he usually tried to be on the phone with someone to avoid talking to her. Beverly had been at a loss as to what to do to make him engage and at least converse with her for a bit.

So today, while she would offer him a smoothie, he would likely turn her down after making a grimace of distaste. Anything except bacon and eggs along with toast and butter and a large cup of orange juice was typically turned down.

He didn't even make an effort to try it when she made anything else for breakfast. She'd tried to lure him to eat with her using several of her mother's tried and true B&B recipes. Muffins,

French toast, breakfast casserole and cinnamon rolls had all been turned down with an expression that told her he considered her mother's recipes akin to peasant food. It was like she had asked him to take a bite out of a raw, still beating heart, torn from the chest of a big beast and dripping blood.

She hadn't done that.

The truth was Beverly knew he felt that way because she'd overheard him tell one of his sisters recently how he felt about her mother's B&B breakfasts. The words "pedestrian" and "greasy" and "bad roadside diner fare" had been mentioned. It wasn't true. Her mother's food was top notch and many in the local foodie world had told her so.

After being basically ignored for the last couple of months, she was ready for a confrontation. Today, she was not going to be Meek Beverly. Today, she was going to force a meaningful conversation out of her husband. Today, she would not be ignored.

Noah came down at a quarter to eight, dressed in his usual suit complete with a smart tie and his briefcase in hand. He used one of their four bedrooms upstairs as a home office. It was another place for him to escape and ignore her each evening. But not any longer.

When Noah rounded the corner to enter the kitchen, he stopped short, his eyes widening, as if he was perpetually surprised to see her. Every day of their marriage, she had been in the kitchen waiting for him. When he came home, she greeted him from the same place in the kitchen as he entered from the garage after watching to ensure the garage door went down and stayed down.

One time, well over a year ago, a leaf or something had blown in as the door closed and their garage had ended up being open all night. Noah had been nearly apoplectic the next day. He blamed her, of course, even though he'd been the only one to leave the house the day before.

And she'd even said to him, "Noah, *you* were the only one to leave the house yesterday."

He'd gruffly replied, "Well, make sure from now on that you check every time you come in and out. I don't want anyone getting in or stealing anything."

Beverly had wanted to say, "Back at you, Bub!" but she hadn't. She had just nodded and tried to get along with him. That was what she usually did, but that was about to change.

Today, Beverly mentally took a deep breath and said, "I made a new smoothie recipe this morning. I think it's very tasty. Would you like to try it?" She pointed to the blender and her yummy purple concoction.

He didn't even say anything. Instead, Noah rolled his eyes at her.

He. Rolled. His. Eyes. At. Her. *Seriously?*

Noah glanced upstairs with a wistful expression. If there had been another way to get to their garage, he likely would have exited the house through his upstairs office window and slid down the nearest gutter downspout to avoid her completely. Right this moment, he was likely considering how mussed his suit would get if he tried it.

From her perspective, it was too late. He'd have to pull up his big boy pants and deal with her whether he liked it or not. *No downspout travel for you, Mister.*

"What is wrong with you, Noah?" Beverly said. She hadn't yelled like she wanted to, but merely asked her question in a calm voice.

Even so, that got his attention. Noah's eyes widened. "I beg your pardon?"

"You heard me! Every morning, for the entirety of our marriage, I've tried to engage you in a conversation and offer you food. You always turn me down, even if I've gone to extra trouble to make your favorite breakfast, instead preferring *club* food to mine. I mean, why are their eggs, bacon, buttered toast and orange juice better than mine? Huh?"

Noah's eyes got even wider and his lips parted. If he was about to say something, it wasn't his turn yet. Beverly had more to say.

"Today you didn't even speak. You just *rolled your eyes at me*, like I'm some sort of obligation you must endure every single day of your life. And then, each night you stroll inside our home, continually surprised to see me still here. I'm your wife, Noah! I live here, too. I'm sick to death of being ignored and living with a hostile roommate. And it has to change one way or another. Today!

Right now!"

He just stood there like a shocked statue, mouth hanging open, but saying nothing. She was willing to admit that her tone of voice had risen to more of a shout by the end of what she said. He remained silent, as if unable to figure out how to exit without making a comment.

"Speak, Noah! Say something to me like I exist!"

"I don't know what to say, Beverly. I thought things were going along just fine."

"Just fine? Are you kidding me? This is the life you expected us to have? From my perspective it is lacking in significant ways."

His surprise was gone, replaced with a look she didn't want to see. It was the one that said he felt superior to whoever he was talking to. She had seen that look many times before, just not directed at her.

Back when Noah used to take Beverly out to office gatherings, club dinners and the like, she'd seen that expression a thousand times. Once the undesirable person in question walked away from them, Noah would always, *always* belittle them. He would say something rude and snicker behind his hand about how that poor guy didn't have a clue about what real men in the real world did.

"I don't understand, Beverly. How is it lacking?"

"How about the fact you never touch me anymore? Ever!" Beverly didn't understand until this second how much that realization hurt most of all. She'd wanted children from the first. Especially after what happened right before they got married.

Noah, on the other hand, wanted to wait until he was more established in his career, but he used to say they could certainly practice for when the time came. They hadn't been practicing anything together intimately since the night she returned from her sister's house two months ago.

His lips formed a thin line, as if he was repulsed by the thought of coming into contact with her in any form or fashion. And that hurt even more. Beverly fought back the tears of rejection that were on their way. She didn't want to cry. He'd interpret it as a weakness. She wasn't. She was determined.

"Perhaps if you made more of an effort, Beverly." His stern look took her aback.

She responded without thinking, "How? What do I need to do to make more of an effort?" Beverly could barely process his superior attitude without wanting to punch the smirk off of his face. He acted like *she* was the problem between them. She wasn't.

He placed his briefcase on the corner of the bar nearest the garage door and approached the opposite end of the island slowly. Beverly had never been afraid of him, but she was uncertain of what he was about to do.

Noah stopped more than an arm's length

away and pushed out a long sigh. "Why don't you go to the club more often? Why don't you engage with my family more? Why are you content to hide out at home continually as if you are a hermit?"

Beverly straightened in her seat. "Because I'm never invited to the club, because your family hates me and wishes we never got married, and because then I don't have to endure the stares of everyone in your circle of friends and your family making me feel like I'm not good enough."

Noah pushed out another long sigh. After a tense staring match she refused to back down from, he asked, "Would you like to come to the club with me this morning for breakfast?"

Beverly took a deep breath, ready to tell him she didn't want to go and to please not make her. Instead, she said, "Yes. Thank you. That would be lovely."

Noah glanced at his gold wrist watch. "Go on up and change, but hurry, okay?"

Beverly thought she was dressed in perfectly fine clothes for a casual breakfast at the club, but made an extra effort to be agreeable and to discover what he considered appropriate. She asked in as seductive of a tone as she could manage, "What would you like me to wear for you?"

He looked surprised again, but said, "I love that yellow dress that we bought for you a few months back."

She smiled, kissed his cheek as she passed him and headed for the stairs, racing up them to change as quickly as possible.

The dress he suggested was very nice. He called it a day dress, she felt it was more like an afternoon party dress at a weekend gathering, but whatever, she was going to grin and bear it.

She'd deal with her dread about the way some of the guests at the club always looked at her. Either like she was an employee, eager and ready to serve their every little need. Or worse, like she was something they wanted to scrape off their expensive shoes and never deal with ever again. Mostly it was just friends of the Peytons' social group and not the general crowd at the club.

Beverly also touched up her makeup, grabbed some yellow shoes and headed for the stairs. That's when she heard the garage door opening. She hurried down the stairs, grabbed her purse and headed for the garage. She opened the door as the garage door started coming down and closing again.

Her cell phone pinged, signaling she had a text. She stopped to reach into her purse and get her phone, but saw out the front window that Noah was already in the driveway, backing his car out onto their quiet street. The sound of the garage door closing made her heartbeat race in shock.

She didn't know what to do. Why was he leaving without her?

Beverly grabbed her cellphone and saw the waiting text message was from Noah.

I couldn't wait for you any longer, Beverly. I

have to get to work early today. Maybe some other time.

He didn't say he was sorry, because likely he wasn't. He just wanted to get out of the house without dealing with her or having an argument. His attitude that *things are just fine as they are*, didn't hold water for her anymore.

She texted back. *Maybe some other time* you *will actually give me a sincere invitation for breakfast, unlike today.* She did not get any further texts from him.

Beverly was so angry she started pacing beside the kitchen island, plotting all manner of horrible things she could do to Noah in order to take him down a notch.

What would work? What could she do? An awful idea swirled around in her head all of a sudden, forming a more solid structure the more she thought about it.

Beverly grabbed her purse, reached in and got her car keys and headed for the garage. The hermit was about to be liberated to inflict havoc on her husband's horrible dismissive and deceptive antics from this morning.

She didn't care if it ruined everything between them.

From her perspective, their relationship, and any hope of repairing it, was already lost.

Chapter Nine

When the time came, Zoe got ready for class, hopped into her car and headed to the campus. It was only twenty minutes away. That was one of the reasons she'd selected the house she had, because it was so close to school. Actually, her and Evan's home was close to lots of things. She loved that their house was centrally located halfway between Cape Canaveral North and Cape Canaveral Beach.

She even found a rare parking spot near the front of the building and decided that was very good luck. It was going to be a great day.

Her class went by quickly, and Zoe was on her way to the advisor's office in the central administrator's building. Professor Angie Lambert was the head of the hotel management and hospitality management departments and one of Zoe's favorite instructors.

"Hi, Professor Lambert," Zoe said once inside her advisor's office.

"Hi, Zoe. I'm so excited that you're finally here."

"I'm not late, am I?" Zoe asked.

"Not at all. You're right on time, as usual." Her expression looked like she clearly had news and was excited to share it with Zoe.

Mentally, Zoe took a deep breath to ready herself for whatever news was about to be shared.

Professor Lambert reached for a packet on her desk and turned to Zoe with a big grin. Clearly, she had some very good news. Zoe didn't have a clue as to what it could be, though.

"Good. What's up? I thought we were just setting up my final couple of classes. Nothing too exciting about that."

"No, not that. Something better." Dr. Lambert practically glowed. "I've got amazing news for you."

"Cool. What's going on?"

"You got it!" Professor Lambert said, clutching the papers in her hand and widening the already big grin on her face.

Zoe smiled back. But she was baffled. "What is it? What did I get?"

"The internship!" Professor Lambert was practically giddy.

Zoe thought, *What internship?* She blinked once and tried to remember why Professor Lambert was so happy and what she was talking about. She figured she'd just do her internship at the Driftwood Inn or perhaps the Lighthouse Inn, if having her mother as her intern director was deemed inappropriate.

"The Ritz-Carleton Biscayne Bay, Miami internship!" Professor Lambert let out a little scream of jubilation. The Ritz-Carleton Biscayne Bay, Miami internship was a very big deal.

"What?!" Zoe was glad she'd been sitting down for this auspicious news. She never expected to get it. Never!

"You beat out forty-nine other contenders, Zoe. I'm so proud of you. You totally deserve this and I'm so happy I get to be the one to tell you about it."

"But I only signed up on a lark. I didn't ever think I'd actually get it." Not a lark really, because even though she didn't think she'd ever get it, the Ritz-Carleton was definitely a big thing. It was the most prestigious and most sought after internship in the whole hospitality management department.

Zoe couldn't quite believe it. But she also knew that Professor Lambert wouldn't punk her like this or say it if it wasn't true. She was literally stunned into silence.

"I know this is a bit unexpected, but congratulations, Zoe. You were the best choice out of all the applicants from this college. Now we know you were the best one from *all* the participating colleges. They absolutely loved your essay on how you grew up in a B&B and how your mother worked so hard and in turn inspired you to continue in the family business. It was truly moving. I may have shed a tear myself, but don't tell anyone."

Zoe laughed. "I would never tell a soul." Her mind was racing. She had signed up for this internship way last semester. She truly had not expected to actually get it.

Even if she hadn't just gotten married, she hadn't expected to have to leave town for her internship. The details of the internship started filtering into her mind. She believed it was for six whole months and she'd have to move to the hotel and live there in Miami. For six whole months! But without Evan? How could she do that? She was glad she hadn't started talking. She wasn't certain what words would come out of her mouth at this bombshell news.

She was equally excited and fearful at the same time.

Zoe wasn't certain what to do. She needed some time to think about everything. What were her options? Did she even have an option? If she said no, she might never work in Florida hospitality ever again. Well, that was probably not true, her mother wouldn't blacklist her, but it certainly wouldn't look good to turn down such a prestigious internship.

For now, it seemed like a rock or a hard place or a cliff dive into oblivion were her only choices. Then again, even as she knew the problems she would face if she actually took this internship, the idea that she'd beat out forty-nine other contenders made her soul sing with satisfied glee.

She wanted to buy a billboard and advertise this boon for the benefit of all those sometimes mean students who'd made her feel like she didn't have what it took to compete in this field of study. Doing an exaggerated nanny-nanny-boo-boo dance as she rubbed their faces in it would be gratifying, but wasn't the undignified sort of thing she'd ever really do. She could definitely think about it, though.

Then the thought of being away from Evan for six months poured water on her internal happy dance and made her soul shrink in dread.

"Um. How long before I have to decide?"

Professor Lambert's glee melted. "Decide what?"

"Whether I take the internship or not."

Professor Lambert looked positively stricken with concern. "But you *have* to take it, Zoe. It's the best internship for a hospitality degree in the state of Florida, maybe in the entire country. You simply *have* to take it." Her professor's face had morphed from concern to anguish at the thought Zoe wouldn't snap up this opportunity and click her heels in glee.

Zoe didn't want to freak her advisor out, but she wasn't certain she would be able to go. She inhaled deeply and exhaled. "This is just so unexpected, Professor Lambert. Of course, I'm excited and grateful to have gotten this internship but—" Zoe paused, trying to figure out what to say.

"But what?" Her professor's expression changed once more to let in the barest hint of hope.

"Well, the thing is, I got married two months

ago and we just bought a house." Zoe tried to be-seech her advisor to understand all the difficulty she faced in making this decision with a new husband and mortgage in the mix. "It's not that I don't want it. Of course, I do. But I never actually planned for it to happen. I thought the odds were, well, little more than zero."

Professor Lambert suddenly relaxed, heaved out a deep sigh, sounding very relieved and smiled. "Listen. I totally understand, Zoe."

"You do?" That was funny. Even Zoe didn't understand her complex feelings about this coming decision.

"I do and there is nothing for you to worry about. You don't have to forsake your new mortgage and try to manage the additional cost of rent in Miami, too. You will be given a place to stay there at the hotel where you're interning. The cost of room and board is included in the internship.

"In fact, you could probably smuggle your husband in for a couple weekends without any problem, but don't make a habit of it. You'll be very busy every day during the week, and your husband being there for longer than a short visit once or twice would likely be frowned on, if not outright disallowed, but I don't want you to worry about any financial concerns. Okay?"

Zoe pasted a smile on her face and nod-ded. "Okay. Thank you, Professor Lambert. I surely didn't want a home foreclosure on my record be-fore I even graduated." *Now if only my husband will be understanding about a six-month separation. Do I even understand it? Not sure yet.*

"Not to worry. The program doesn't start for a couple of months, so you'll have plenty of time to make arrangements." She handed Zoe the contact information and several forms she'd have to fill out. *The job is never done until the paperwork is finished*, as her mother was fond of saying.

Zoe glanced at the cover page with the official offer, noting that she had to "accept" the internship offer in a week, or sooner would be better. Sigh. So little time to decide!

"Again, I want to offer my heartfelt congratulations, Zoe. You truly deserve this. I'm so delighted for you. I know you'll do a great job and when you do, there may even be a permanent offer extended. I've seen it happen before."

"Thank you, Professor Lambert. This is amazing news." Zoe kept the fake smile plastered on her face until she got back out to her car. A permanent offer to live in Miami was nowhere near what she wanted to do with her life. How could she take over the Driftwood Inn if she was living in Miami working for a hotel? How could she even tell her mother about this new tangle in her life?

Once tucked inside her vehicle with the air conditioning running full blast, Zoe flipped through the paperwork and slumped in her seat. Six months away from Evan would seem like an eternity. What was she going to do?

She decided her best course of action was

to go talk to her mother. She'd know what to do, wouldn't she? Zoe put her car in gear and headed in that direction. Sometimes, you just needed to talk to your mother.

But as Zoe drove to the Driftwood Inn for the afternoon meeting, something else occurred to her. Even if her mother was completely understanding about the internship, Miranda Cole was about to do an extensive expansion of the Driftwood Inn. She had wanted Zoe to be on the premises to help out during the construction phase for the next eight months.

With two months of prep time to get ready to leave, followed by a six-month internship, Zoe wouldn't be back at the Driftwood Inn until the addition was complete and they were hosting the annual Christmas party in the new space. Zoe wouldn't be part of any of the decision-making for the renovation or any of the plans made for after it was complete.

Zoe sighed. Maybe her mother wasn't a good choice of confidant in this particular matter. She took a personal vow of silence and decided against telling her mother anything about the internship until she figured out what she was going to do.

Telling Evan was going to be difficult enough. Even discussing it with him would be hard. He'd probably be supportive whatever she chose, but this great news sure had bad timing.

Zoe decided she'd have to pull up her big girl

pants, as her mother was *also* fond of saying, and figure it out. She'd have to decide whether to take this internship or not, all on her own.

She would also have to make the decision in less than a week; sooner would be the politically correct thing to do. While they'd given her a whole week to accept or decline, it wasn't good form to slide in the day of the expiration to tell them either yes, she'd begrudgingly go or no, start getting the paperwork ready for your second choice candidate.

Zoe had never felt more alone in her life.

Today had started out with such promise, but now Zoe was dreading her coming conversation with Evan and dreading even more the one she'd have to have with her mother.

Zoe let out a long sigh, burdened by the weight of adult decision-making firmly pressing down on her shoulders.

Chapter Ten

Miranda finished her bowl of delicious soup. Her stomach settled down and stopped growling in protest. She glanced at her watch, knowing she had plenty of time to do what she needed to without leaping up right now. She took a deep breath, let it out and then did it again. She calmed down a bit. That was good. She needed to settle down and take things in stride, like she always did.

She did not need to add stress to her day by jumping up and running crazy until she crashed and burned. She was allowed to take a few minutes for herself, wasn't she? Of course, she was. She took another deep breath and let it out. Good. She could feel more stress seep out as she continued to simply breathe in and out, doing her best not to think about all the stressors in her life.

The bistro waitress stopped by her table and asked if Miranda wanted another bowl a soup. Miranda, who had planned to gulp down something and then race on to her next task, decided she deserved to sit and enjoy a quiet, stress-free lunch. Miranda nodded to the waitress, who then asked if she wanted to try their special bean and ham soup variety this time.

Miranda nodded and asked for a small bowl, not ready to leave the quiet of the back table she'd been assigned. It was tucked away around the corner from the main aisle of the bar and table tops through the restaurant space. She needed a break from the craziness of her life for just a few minutes. She had the time in this rare instance.

The new soup variety was delicious, making her wish she'd ordered the larger bowl. The bean and ham soup was served with a small piece of cornbread and honey butter. Delicious.

Miranda's building loan for the expansion at the Driftwood had been given and approved based on the fact that she had most of the money already in the savings account at the bank where her loan originated.

She'd spent several years saving up every penny of it, knowing that if she could expand and add just six more rooms to the Driftwood Inn, the profit from that expansion would enable her to retire in less than ten years. She might even press it and retire in eight if it was at all possible. Time would tell.

She loved her B&B, but one day she planned to step down and spend her time with grandchildren and family. It was one thing to work hard until you dropped dead. It was another to hang it up in a timely manner and enjoy the waning years of your life. Miranda chose door number two and was doing her best to set that dream in motion with her expansion plan.

Miranda worked hard, but she did not consider herself a workaholic. She liked to think she knew when the right time would be to hand over her B&B and slow things down. Surrounding herself with grandchildren was what she considered the best way to spend her retirement years.

She had hoped to start this renovation project earlier, like a few years earlier. Unfortunately, Bill's income had not increased in the last several years. At one time, her husband had contributed a third of his salary to their savings account, after the bills were paid, then only a fourth. Eventually, it became sporadic deposits only a few times a year. Lately, not a penny. In fact, not a single cent in over eight years, when she went back in her files to look.

While he'd been employed at the same bank for quite a long time, whatever income he received hadn't gone into their joint account or their savings for almost a decade. Since he went out of his way not to talk about work, she wondered if his status had changed again. She hoped not, for his sake.

His dwindling income over the past decade was yet another thing they didn't talk about. Ever. She'd tried, but had been put off, ignored, and the last time she mentioned it a few years ago, he'd been rather hostile in his determination not to discuss it.

So, she let it go, like she'd let so many other things go, until now there wasn't much left between them to discuss. They were the very definition of growing apart. Miranda thought Bill's transformation into the sullen Plastic William had more to do with them having nothing in common anymore, but there were other issues.

Bill had once been a fairly popular loan officer where he worked, but starting around ten years ago, it seemed like the bank started cutting back on staffing. Maybe they'd just cut back on Bill's workload and job responsibilities. He never seemed concerned about it, so Miranda didn't press him. In fact, the one time she asked him about his title change when they used to talk about such things, he seemed quite embarrassed, so she let it go. Again. At least then she'd let it go because she loved him and didn't want to make him feel bad, not because it was easier than confronting him.

Five years ago, he'd announced he'd become a senior account manager, whatever that was. His salary deposits into their bank account became even more infrequent and the phrase "working on commission" came up in a conversation Miranda overheard at a holiday party.

Two years later, she saw new business cards he'd ordered and learned he'd become simply an account manager, losing the *senior* part of his job title.

Losing the title hadn't mattered to Bill as

much as losing his private office and his private assistant. He'd been extremely upset about losing what he felt he'd earned for being so loyal to the bank for so many years. Clearly his employer had not agreed.

As she thought about it, his loss of status at work had happened around the same time as Beverly's wedding. Looking back with a more critical eye, she wondered if someone at the bank was related to Noah's family and if that was why Bill had been so adamant about his non-support of his daughter's choice of husband.

Miranda had attributed Bill's poor attitude over that festive event to his lowered change of status at work, but now she wasn't so sure. She'd overheard a stranger at the wedding reception talking to someone else she didn't know about a possible rivalry between the Coles and the Peytons like the Hatfields and McCoys. At the time, she'd thought they were drunk.

It was sort of sad to realize she was getting her best information about her husband's career from overheard tidbits and snippets of conversation between strangers at social events.

She didn't know what rivalry there might be between Bill and the Peyton family that existed beyond Beverly being pregnant and the semi-shotgun wedding aspect of the union. The plans for the wedding had come together in a couple of months rather than over a year, but she certainly didn't harbor the same resentment Bill did. And he'd never truly explained why his attitude had been so absolute and negative about Beverly's union to Noah.

Recently, Bill had floated the idea of going down to part-time at the bank. Miranda had told him in no uncertain terms that was absolutely not going to happen, and that from her perspective that would be a big fat no. Not surprisingly, he'd been resentful about it.

She reminded him that their health insurance was dependent on him having a full-time job. Unless he was going somewhere else to get another full-time job with insurance benefits, he could sit his butt at the bank and be grateful they kept him on. Miranda remembered Bill's expression as being rather insolent.

Once Miranda finished eating her second bowl of delicious soup, she lingered in the bistro, thinking about Bill and what her new awesome lawyer told her this morning, even though they'd only met briefly. She ordered a second glass of iced tea and mulled over her life in general and what she wanted, what she expected, and then what she was likely going to get in the end.

She glanced at her watch and realized she needed to quit woolgathering and get to the store. Taking a stress break was one thing, day-dreaming for over an hour was another. Even so, taking these few minutes of quiet time had calmed her considerably. She felt better about life in general. She would go forward with her head up and do her best to meet any challenges that came her way.

Her meeting with Theo Jackson was in two hours. She was very excited about it. They were meeting at the Driftwood Inn conference room, so they'd have room to spread out all the blueprints and elevation plans. She was couldn't wait to get started on this long-awaited project.

It took her several years to save up enough to put her dream renovation in motion. She had to secure a business loan for the expenditure, but most of the money she needed was tucked away in her savings account. Even so, any loan interest she paid would be a business expense for taxes.

Miranda paid her lunch bill with cash, leaving a good tip. The service in this bistro was amazing. She would definitely come back.

She stopped by the bathroom to freshen up and then strolled through the busy restaurant, walking parallel to the ornate carved wooden bar on one side of the place and outside into the warm spring day. She planned to walk to the grocery store, do her shopping and then head back to the Driftwood Inn with her groceries tucked in the trunk. It was going to be busy starting next week, but she got another thrill at the prospect of her expansion breaking ground soon.

The upscale bistro had an outdoor area where several guests were eating lunch al fresco at small tables under large umbrellas. As she made her way between the tables, she saw the partial profile of a man with jet-black hair seated across from a very young woman. Their hands on the table were clasped, and the way he stroked the back of her hand with his thumb was in no way fatherly.

She didn't recognize him right away, but he looked familiar. In fact, his clothing looked like something her husband owned. Were there really two men with such poor taste in clothing living in Canaveral Beach North?

Then the man turned and she stopped moving. Miranda froze in place, realizing that the man with the jet-black hair and poor taste in clothing *was* her husband. And he was having lunch with a very young woman who was not one of their daughters. What was he thinking?

The girl suddenly giggled and Bill threw back his head with the new, odd-looking dyed hair and also laughed. Miranda couldn't move. A couple behind her had to scoot sideways past her in single file because she was stunned into place and seemingly unable to move.

A waiter asked, "Are you okay, ma'am?"

"Yes. Thank you. I am now."

The waiter returned back inside the bistro as she finally shook from her statue stance, gathered her wits about her and marched over to Bill's table.

"Bill?" she said, in an overloud and overly surprised tone. "Fancy meeting you here." Bill's eyes widened to the size of dinner plates and his mouth dropped open.

Miranda turned to the young woman and

said, "Hi, I'm Miranda Cole, Bill's wife. And your name is?" She shot her hand in the girl's direction to shake, even though she didn't want to. She also leaned in close to get a better look at her. First thought, *She's* really *young. Is she out of her teens yet?*

"Oh. Um. Hi. I'm Kaylee," she said, extending a pale, skinny hand and giving Miranda a limp shake with the tips of her fingers.

"You don't have to talk to her, Kaylee," Bill said. "And I go by William now. Why can't you remember that, Miranda?"

Oh, I'm the problem in this situation? I don't think so, Bub.

Miranda turned to him and said, "Well, Elvis, I guess I call you that because you've been called Bill since I met you more than thirty years ago!"

Bill's face turned tomato-red in an instant. "Your attitude is uncalled for, Miranda," he said from between gritted teeth. She noted that his face hadn't moved at all during the conversation.

He looked like a pathetic old man with a plastic face, trying to pretend he was younger than he was. The new jet-black dye job made him look even more ridiculous than she thought was possible.

And it wasn't like Miranda was against plastic surgery if used sensibly. She simply disapproved of drastic changes and false-looking overdone faces. Like Bill's.

What made her so against what Bill or rather "William" was doing, was that he seemed to be trying to change into a different person. Like he wanted to erase his current life, change his face, hair and clothing to become someone completely different. Someone *she* would never be interested in. Someone completely opposite of the man she'd married and been happy and in love with for many years.

Miranda was incensed when she found out what happened with Bill and their youngest son, Gabe, a few weeks ago, after most of his plastic surgery was completed.

Her son would never have told her the story, but someone she trusted overheard it as it happened. Shocked at the way Bill treated Gabe, that person relayed the incident to Miranda.

Apparently, Gabe saw his dad at another restaurant in town and waved when he entered.

Bill very obviously pretended not to see him. He'd looked away and studied his menu, bringing it up to hide the upper part of his body.

Gabe thought maybe he hadn't seen him and didn't approach his father's table.

Then when Bill and his guest got up to leave and passed by the table Gabe was at with some of his friends, he said, "Hey, Dad," as his father walked by. Again, his father said nothing.

Bill not only didn't acknowledge his own son with even a smile, he ignored him completely and walked out of the restaurant like Gabe was some weird stranger who said, "Hey, Dad" to everyone he met.

When Miranda asked Bill for an explanation, she expected him to say something like, "I didn't see him." But no. Instead, he said, "I can't very well look as young as I do now in front of important clients and then say, 'Hi, son,' to an adult man like Gabe, now can I?"

Miranda wanted to slap him across the face to shake him out of this I-want-to-be-twenty-again foolishness. If he was willing to forsake his own son, his own blood, then Miranda knew she wouldn't rate high on his list of priorities, either.

And clearly with the revelation Bill's teen-age-girlfriend lunch date, the priorities had shifted more than even Miranda imagined.

"You aren't qualified to judge anyone's atti-tude, William," Miranda said. "Your disrespect and snootiness toward even your own children in the light of turning *sixty* next year has clearly warped you beyond recognition."

Bill stood up the moment the word sixty came out of her mouth. "Shut up, Miranda! Just shut your big mouth for once in your life!" he shouted loud enough that several other patrons turned to look at them.

"What's wrong, William? Doesn't your teen-age date know how old you really are?" Miranda was so angry she hardly knew what to do. But she decided quickly she needed to express herself.

Miranda turned to Kaylee. "Stay with William if you want, because I'm surely through with him. But you've been forewarned about his impulsive and changeable nature." The girl's eyes widened but she remained silent. That was likely a good thing. Miranda stepped back, shook her head to rid herself of the incident, but unable to ignore the disgust she felt with her husband and the life path he was on.

Miranda didn't look at Bill or Kaylee as she left the bistro's outdoor eating area and headed straight for the grocery store.

She walked around for several minutes before even realizing where she was and what she was looking for. She stopped in front of a bin of lemons and limes, took a deep breath and let it out. Then she did it again to get her anger under control.

She had been refusing to admit the obvious. Perhaps it was way past time to change *her* life path as Bill had done with such ease. If Bill didn't want to be married to her or acknowledge their children in public, Miranda was going to change her life, as well. And even in her mental discussions, she refused to call him William from now on and she would take pleasure in calling him Bill in person whenever she had to talk to him.

While she was in the frozen foods section, she thought of the business card of the divorce lawyer Roberta had recommended. When she'd gone in to make an appointment and briefly seen Monica Allendale, Miranda had told her the general issue and scheduled an appointment for the following week. That was when she thought she had the luxury of time.

Digging in her wallet, she finally found what she was looking for. She pulled out her new lawyer's business card, dialed the number on her cellphone. When she got Monica Allendale on the line, she said, "This is Miranda Cole. I've just learned new information and I'm going forward with the divorce. I want it done as soon as possible. Are you able to start the paperwork before our first official meeting?"

"Yes, of course. I can begin the paperwork immediately," her awesome new lawyer said. "I'll begin drawing up the necessary documents and we can discuss them. I can get your signature on the necessary papers and we can move forward then."

"Excellent. Thank you very much, Monica." Miranda couldn't wait to hear about the next steps to dissolve her marriage to a man who had become a different person.

Miranda glanced at her watch and hurried to make her grocery purchases so she could get home and put them away.

She wasn't late or anything, but she decided quickly that she needed more time to settle down before her meeting with Theo Jackson. She didn't want to be in a rant and rave mood. Theo didn't deserve it.

Her husband, on the other hand, was about to discover that where *he* was concerned, her only discussion mood settings were going to be either rant or rave. His choice.

Chapter Eleven

Beverly was out for blood. Specifically, she wanted Noah's blood. How dare he invite her to breakfast and then distract her with some foolishness about changing her perfectly acceptable outfit and promptly ditch her once she was out of sight?

Well, he *had* found a better way to exit the house than crawling out his office window and shimmying down the nearest gutter downspout to avoid her. She give him props for that. However, his actions were beyond the pale as far as she was concerned, a bridge too far in their already fragile relationship. And she wouldn't stand for it. Not this time.

Beverly wanted vengeance. His foolish action demanded it. Noah was about to understand what she was willing to do in the name of retribution. And she was about to render it to him personally. She wasn't certain exactly all the things she planned to do, but first up was telling him how she felt and ensuring he understood her anger over his stunt.

She drove with quiet purpose to the country

club where Noah and his family practically lived as a second home and was stopped at the gate.

Beverly didn't have a special sticker on her car allowing her immediate entrance to the country club grounds. However, unless Noah had changed something today, she should be able to flash her ID and get inside. She was likely still on the list of approved guests. Today might be her last welcome day.

"Hi. I'm meeting my husband Noah Peyton for breakfast," she said with a big smile.

The gate guard didn't smile in return. He wrote down her license plate number, glanced at her ID and checked his computer before letting a small curve of his lips to register. "Have a nice day, ma'am," he said and raised the gate for her to drive through.

"Thank you!" she said with a huge smile. The guard narrowed his eyes, but then smiled back as she practically burned rubber getting inside the country club's gates.

Beverly drove through quickly before a red alert from the main country club offices came through, banning her forever. That would certainly be the result of whatever she did today.

The special, "Thank you," to the gate guard was something she usually would not do because Noah and his snobby family thought it was also pedestrian of her to want to be gracious to service staff and not what rich folks did. It was something they frowned on every time she accidently *forgot* and thanked some hapless waiter, host or water-pouring staff member.

Their theory was that if they had to say thank you for everything, they'd say it all day long, and that would never do.

At least that was what she'd been told by several members of the Peyton family, starting with each of Noah's four older sisters, his mother and a couple of aunts who were visiting from an out-of-town snotty country club.

They'd all told her more than once. It was difficult for her to have someone do something nice for her and not at least whisper a thank-you. Clearly Noah's relatives thought she'd been brought up wrong. And that was only the first in a long list of transgressions she made each and every day.

Beverly thought of it as the *411 on basic treatment of lesser people*. Even though she'd heard other club members thank various staff, the Peytons never did. Ever. For her to do so not only broke the code of their family, it also made them look bad for being so stingy with their praise in the small things.

As Beverly's mother always said, "If you can't even be trusted to do the little things, how can you earn trust to do the big things in this world?"

Clearly, if you were rich, the rules were different. That was the only thing Beverly had learned in her time as a barely tolerated member of the Peyton family. Part of her was delighted to be burning emotional bridges today. She would glee-fully set fire to all the foolishness Noah and his family had demanded of her. It didn't matter. They never allowed her into the clique no matter what she did.

This morning a bell sounded like a gong in her mind. *This stuffy, abominable attitude that you hate so much will last a lifetime unless you stop it. No more!*

She was about to speak her mind, tell Noah how she felt and let the chips fall where they may.

Beverly drove slowly along the nicely paved, smooth road to the parking lot near the club din-ing room. She pulled into a spot marked for guests, even though she had an assigned place closer to the door.

She didn't want Noah to know she'd fol-lowed him here. Not yet. She was fairly vibrat-ing with fury, wanting to burn his world to the ground. But she took a page from her mother's book on anger.

Miranda Cole told all of her children to count to ten before saying anything they'd regret. Get a good night's sleep before responding to something online or in the mail that made you angry. And most of all, "Don't ever let anyone know you are plotting revenge. Be sneaky and plan for it in order to get better results and satisfaction." Her mother was a very smart woman.

Beverly walked to the host station in front of the dining room. The man there pretended she was invisible for a full minute before she cleared her throat and got his attention.

"Yes," he said, not looking directly at her.

"Is my husband Noah Peyton in the dining room? I wasn't sure I'd make it in time for us to eat together, but I hope so," she said in such a sweet tone, room temperature butter wouldn't melt in her mouth.

The guy practically choked when she said Noah's name, and changed his lofty tone in a hurry.

"Why, yes, Mrs. Peyton. Mr. Peyton is in the Cyprus Room this morning." He snapped his fingers and a young man with slicked back hair and dressed it the club's chic red and white uniform arrived.

The young man listened to a whispered instruction from the host, looked over one shoulder at her to ensure she would follow, and started walking to the Cyprus Room.

Beverly followed, but stayed a good four feet behind him. Wouldn't want to accidentally bump into a lesser servant person if they stopped too quickly. Mentally, Beverly rolled her eyes at the pompousness she'd endured for the whole of her marriage.

They walked through an empty room filled with tables that looked like they were set for a fancy dinner and past a two-story entryway leading into an area where breakfast was served. There was also a third room she'd been to once that was for luncheon only.

And there was *never* a buffet. The horror of all horrors. No. They might as well sit on the floor and eat with their fingers rather than endure a buffet. In no uncertain terms would that ever happen in the club's dining room. Uniformed service people catered to every need for the club's members and guests. That's what they paid for, not a buffet where they had to serve themselves. They'd rather starve.

Back when she and Noah had been deliriously in love, Beverly had been so impressed the first time she'd been here. She'd tried to be on her best behavior. As with her whole tenure in the Peyton family, it hadn't been close to good enough.

Later, every miniscule mistake she'd made was pointed out to her, repeatedly. Like saying thank you to the wait staff who did anything for her during the entire evening. Or like not scolding a girl filling her wine glass who allowed a single drop to soil the tablecloth next to her napkin. It had been a wonder they hadn't ordered the table cleared for the transgression and fired the server after having her flogged in the public square.

Beverly saw the look one of Noah's older sisters, Lina, sent her way during what Beverly privately referred to as that evening's premier wine drop debacle. Hatred had glowered out of Lina's gaze as she stared at the wine server and the same look had promptly spilled over to Beverly when she tried to comfort the girl. Lina's scowl came with an imperious finish, shaking her head slightly as she stared endlessly until Beverly decided to look away, unsure of what she'd done to earn such malice.

Beverly had been surprised by the venom in Lina's stare, but then saw it repeated by several other members of the Peyton family. First at the wine server for being clumsy, then at Beverly for daring to be nice to her. Of course, her greatest transgression was daring to be involved with their only son, Noah.

She was glad it had been at the end of the meal, because they left soon after and Beverly understood clearly how Noah's family truly felt about the likes of her.

Finding out she was pregnant a week later had been many parts of wretched fear about how the Peyton family would react versus how her parents would respond to the news. That was a week of hellish stress that she never wanted to repeat in her life. She was likely about to test that here in a few minutes by poking an already annoyed Noah.

The attendant with the slicked-back hair led her directly to Noah's table. He was sipping coffee as he read a newspaper, not paying attention to his surroundings. Why would he? He thought he was dining alone this morning.

"Mr. Peyton," the slick-haired attendant said. "Your wife is here."

"What?" Noah dropped his paper on the table as his coffee cup wobbled within his grasp.

He managed to hold onto the cup, but a dribble of coffee swirled out to splash onto his fancy place-mat.

He stood up as if he'd just drenched himself in coffee but he was just being overly dramatic to make the attendant feel bad. He looked at the slick-haired attendant and gave him a scowl mean enough to make the guy blanch

Beverly had to work hard not to roll her eyes at what she'd always referred to as the entitled performance of put-upon-ness all members of the Peyton clan had mastered. Servants across the country club likely cowered in fear, quit their jobs, changed their names and were never heard from again after receiving a look like that.

Beverly stepped between them, heading for the chair opposite her husband.

"Hi, honey," Beverly said in a singsong voice like she called him that every day. She didn't.

Noah was momentarily distracted, so she added, "I'm glad I got here before you ordered."

She promptly kissed Noah's cheek, diverting his attention from the slick-haired attendant, who scurried away in a hurry after realizing he'd given Mr. Peyton unexpected and clearly not very good news. Smart boy. Although he'd probably never be heard from again.

"What in the world are you doing here, Beverly?" Noah asked, clearly stunned by her appearance. You would have thought she had pranced in here naked except for her pricy yellow shoes and matching pocketbook.

"I was invited," she responded brightly. She seated herself across from him, with help from a waiter who seemingly appeared out of nowhere.

Another attendant was already removing the barely soiled placemat to replace it with a new one, including fresh silverware. Gracious, Noah sure had them all jumping in fear over the slightest of problems.

This was the life her husband and his entire entitled family adored. She realized in this moment how much she truly hated it. She loathed treating people who served her like they were no better than the dirt on the bottom of her shoes. The Peyton family reveled in treating people who served them, in any form or fashion, like trash.

Noah stood there with his drippy coffee cup and stared at her in shock. The attendant took his cup from his fingers gently and placed a clean cup on the table, filling it from what was surely a freshly brewed pot of the finest coffee money could buy.

Her husband suddenly came to from his winning put-upon-ness performance, cleared his throat and sat back down, scooting his chair in. He didn't say anything, but she could tell his brain was working overtime to figure out what to do in this unprecedented situation.

Beverly, feeling particularly vengeful, said, "Thank you so much!" to the waiter who'd taken basically only thirty seconds to replace everything in front of Noah because he dropped one spot of coffee on his placemat.

The waiter smiled and scurried away like the others, clearly understanding that Noah was not going to say thank you.

Noah glared at her. "I told you I didn't have time today. You took too long changing clothes."

"About that. Why did you make me change clothes? If you were in a hurry, the dress I had on before was perfectly acceptable for breakfast here." His eyes narrowed, as if he couldn't believe she would dare question him. She smiled as if she didn't have a care in the world.

"I disagree," he said curtly, scanning the new placemat, probably to ensure it was ironed flat enough for him. Not seeing an obvious flaw, he grunted once and picked up his fresh coffee in the new cup and took a sip.

"Well, we'll have to agree to disagree on that score," she said brightly.

Noah's eyes darted in her direction. She forced her smile. His expression tightened, as if he realized some unfamiliar game was afoot and he didn't know how to play nor did he want to.

Too bad, she thought. This day had been a long time in coming.

Two months ago they'd had a fight that sent her to her sister's for a break. When Beverly returned, upon his seemingly sincere admission that he missed her and wanted her to come home, it didn't take long to realize that nothing they'd disagreed on was ever going to change. The reasons she'd left had been monumental to her, but for Noah, it was clearly back to business as usual.

In fact, with the way he scurried out the door every morning and ignored her when he was at home, things were even worse than before their brief separation.

Beverly studied her husband. He was very handsome. She'd always thought so. She couldn't believe it when he asked her out. She'd jumped at the chance to be with such a popular boy at school. It was possible he'd only asked her out to anger his sisters or his parents and date someone unacceptable, but he seemed happy when they were together in their early days. Back when he wasn't such a pompous idiot. Alas, the newness of disobeying his family and marrying someone lesser had worn off. And now that he was out of school and worked in the Peytons' banking business, he spent much more time with his family. Loads more than when they'd met. It didn't take long for him to turn into a rich robot snob just like them.

Noah took the opportunity to glance around the room as if to assess what other snobby people might see him as he was forced to share a table with his unacceptable wife.

A waiter who certainly didn't understand the power struggle transpiring between them came to the table, bent at the waist and asked Beverly, "What would you like to drink, ma'am?"

"I'll have coffee with cream, please." She

didn't look at Noah, but figured he was probably still pouting over her unexpected arrival. So be it.

The waiter handed her a menu and departed. Beverly opened it up, ignoring Noah, and scanned the first page. By the time she'd made her selection, the waiter was back with her coffee.

He placed a small, white porcelain pitcher filled with cream alongside her coffee cup, which he filled from a pot that had probably been brewed less than five minutes before.

"Thank you so much," she said with a smile when he lifted the pot up.

The waiter smiled back and asked, "What would madam like for breakfast this morning?"

Beverly kept her attention on the waiter, purposely *not* looking at any possible foul looks Noah might be shooting in her direction. "I'll have the eggs Benedict with hash browns on the side and an order of fresh fruit, please."

"Very good, madam."

"Thank you," she said to him once more. Their waiter smiled at her and she noted his surprise at her saying something kind before he turned and walked away.

Noah waited until the man was out of earshot before whispering tersely, "Beverly, you are embarrassing me. What is wrong with you?"

"Nothing is wrong with me, Noah." She gave him a serene look that he did not return. "I'm not sure I understand why you would think that." She knew.

"You do too know why. Stop it."

Beverly leaned forward and hissed, "No. Please explain, Noah. How am I embarrassing you? Huh? Because I said thank-you to someone who did something for me. Too bad. Get over it. I'm not going to stop giving verbal gratitude to people who do things for me. "

He tilted his head to one side as if he were speaking to someone who didn't understand the language he spoke. After several moments of Beverly staring as he was apparently trying to think of what to say to her, he breathed out a long breath.

"It's clear to everyone in the club that you do not belong here. I think you should finish quickly and leave."

"I disagree. And so you can prepare yourself, I plan to take my time and have a delicious breakfast here at the club. My husband says I should come here more often. So I'm going to," she said. Noah didn't look at her, but she saw his jaw clench. *Bingo.*

Beverly watched him. He didn't deign to look at her, so she sat back in her chair and viewed the room around them like she was an awestruck tourist, admiring the fancy decorations. It would make him furious and she knew it. And she really worked extra hard to make him especially irate at this, surely final, breakfast together at the club.

"Beverly," he said her name quietly between clenched teeth. "Stop what you are doing."

"Or else what," she said without looking at

him. "Are you going to scream at me or strike me in public for daring to look around the room?" He didn't say a word. "I didn't think so."

Beverly didn't stop searching the room, blatantly staring at the ceiling with the ornate craftsmanship formed in the plaster, the walls filled with all manner of beautiful paintings and the lovely tapestries that graced the walls in the overly large and tall room. Someone should take the time to look at them, she figured. Someone had gone to a lot of expense to make this room look like it was fit for royalty.

She looked behind her at the beautiful tapestry on the wall. When she finally turned around to face Noah, she was surprised his face wasn't flushed red, with the vein in his forehead bulging with the beat of his cold, snobby heart.

Instead, he had picked up his newspaper and started reading it again. He lifted his freshly poured cup of coffee to his lips and sipped it. The message was obvious. He'd decided that the best way to handle her was to ignore her.

Wasn't he going to be in for a surprise when that didn't work?

She knew for a fact that Noah was very perturbed that she'd ordered hash browns with her breakfast. He told her regularly that hash browns were only for trashy people and should only be served in low-life diners along busy highways or at grimy buffet tables feeding masses of the poor.

Beverly disagreed. Hash browns were delicious sides for any possible occasion. Potatoes in any form were food of the gods as far as she was concerned.

She cleared her throat, but Noah didn't look at her. He continued scanning his newspaper, trying to look like he was reading it. She suspected he was just being a snot.

"Are you going to pretend I'm not here, Noah? If so, that's really foolish." Beverly told him this in a civil, quiet tone, but she didn't plan to keep her voice low if he was going to act like a petulant child the whole time they were together.

He didn't respond or react. Beverly pushed out a mental sigh and thought about what she could do to stir things up. What could she do to *really* push him over the edge? She'd have to think about it for a few minutes.

First, though, she was going to enjoy her breakfast. The smoothie she'd made this morning was good, but not filling. Besides, eggs Benedict was her favorite. And the hash browns here at the club were amazing with a capital A. She would enjoy them even more, knowing that Noah would disapprove of every bite she took. *I even know what I'll do to really drive home my unhappiness over what you did this morning.*

Beverly planned to moan in delight with every bite of hash brown she chewed. She wondered if that would finally push Noah to actually talk to her and stop pretending she wasn't here.

If that didn't get him to acknowledge her,

perhaps she'd start a loud conversation with the nice older couple being seated at the next table. That might actually do it. She'd push him right over the edge and see what he did. She couldn't wait.

However, if Noah did anything ill-mannered to her person, she would at least have witnesses. That might be very important if she kept up her vengeful actions throughout breakfast.

And she planned to do just that.

Revenge might be a dish best served cold, but Beverly thought perhaps it should be served with hash browns that tasted like heaven and de-manded a little moan of delight with each bite.

Chapter Twelve

Zoe sat in her car, waiting for the red light to turn green so she could go home and ponder her day. It had gone by in a blur, especially after talking to her college advisor and hearing the announcement of the big news.

After she left the advisor's office, Zoe went to the meeting at the Driftwood Inn to talk final plans before they broke ground on her mother's expansion project. Zoe mostly kept quiet, afraid she'd blurt out that while she was here for the beginning of the project, she would not be around for the final six months of it, maybe longer.

Luckily, the meeting was short and Zoe was able to escape to head back to campus for a study group she had forgotten about. To her credit, she'd put an alert on her phone so she wouldn't forget and miss it, since it was at an unusual time late in the afternoon.

After her study group, which broke up early because several others had a big test in some class she'd taken last semester, Zoe stayed on campus. She didn't really need to, but managed to kill time and avoid going home for a few hours. She went to the bookstore to browse, getting a snack and something to drink, since she'd missed lunch after the big news from her professor. She didn't remember much of the specifics of her day, even as she finally got around to heading home.

As she'd thought about all day long, Zoe pondered all the issues this one-of-a-kind, life-changing internship in Miami would bring. She also acknowledged that deep down inside, she *wanted* to take it. She truly deserved it.

Turning down the internship in Miami would be akin to quitting a project after working for a very long time to achieve an important goal and then walking away, never to return to that which she'd sweated and worked so hard for in the first place.

She simply couldn't bring herself to do it. *I'm not a quitter*, she told herself, as if she needed reminding. She didn't.

Besides, saying no to this prestigious internship was really not a good idea for her career. What if it impacted her hospitality career for the rest of her life? Twenty years from now, strangers would see her, walk around her as if she were a leper and whisper behind their hands, "That's Zoe Pierce! You know! The sap who turned down the most prestigious hotel internship in the country because she was afraid to tell her husband and her mommy about it." It was a foolish scenario that wouldn't ever happen, but she added it to the long list of regrets she'd have if she didn't take this auspicious and well-earned boon.

Zoe pondered how severely these issues would impact her life in general. And it meant that she needed to figure out a way to tell Evan and have him be okay with her ditching him for six months, possibly longer, if they offered her a job. She decided to burn the "hey, they offered me a job to stay in Miami" bridge down when she came to it and not a second sooner.

A horn honked behind her and she noted that the light had turned green. She pressed the gas pedal slowly, suddenly not in a hurry to get home.

She wasn't certain what Evan would say. She didn't have a single inkling. He totally supported her going to school and finishing her degree. But she also knew how important Evan's business was to him. It wasn't like he ran his hardware store from home and could pick up and travel to Miami with her, even if the hotel *would* let her bring him along for more than a couple of weekends.

How could she pass on this amazing offer? Well, she couldn't. How could she convince Evan to be delighted with her absence for so long? She didn't want to. Therefore, no good choices were available so far.

It was simple. Say yes or no. Accept or decline. Tell Evan and explain your feelings.

Her brain was practically smoking as she thought hard and long about her dismal simple choices.

Zoe pulled her car into the driveway, realizing she would have to tell Evan and let the chips fall wherever they landed. Either way, there was likely to be a big mess to clean up.

Evan greeted her with a kiss as she came inside their home. That was odd. Not that he kissed her, but that he beat her home. Was he early or was she late?

"What time is it?" she said, looking over her shoulder at the decorative wall clock they'd picked out together in a small coastal town a few miles from Cape Canaveral Beach. That was when she realized she was over an hour late coming home. Huh? She must have been at the library longer than she thought while her brain worked overtime chewing on this problem.

Or perhaps she'd taken a really long time to drive home. Or perhaps both things were true. Maybe she needed to unburden herself, share her news with Evan so her brain could function correctly.

Evan grinned. "It's later than you usually get home o'clock. I was about to send out the search dogs." He looked really happy. She hoped this evening's discussion wouldn't change that.

"You have search dogs?" she asked and gave him a rueful look of disbelief combined with a smile that said she was sorry to be late without calling. It was a wonder she made it home at all. She really needed to talk to Evan, make a decision and give her brain a rest.

Her question made him chuckle. "Well, no," he admitted. "But I do have an extensive family phone tree that includes three sisters and an attentive mother, and I'm not afraid to use it. Because they will all do their best to hunt you down and bring you back to me. Count on it."

Zoe laughed and hugged her husband close. "I love you, Mr. Pierce. Sorry I'm late. I would have called if I'd realized the time."

"I love you, too, Mrs. Pierce. No worries. Or is this a sly way to have me buy you a new watch?"

"Very funny. I'm not that sly."

"Then tell me, Mrs. Pierce, where have you been and how was your day?"

She almost replied with her big news, but couldn't get the words out. She wasn't ready to share. Not quite yet.

Zoe didn't know what to do, but the minute she told Evan she wouldn't be able to take the words back if things went awry. She had mapped out no less than ten different *what if* scenarios for breaking the bombshell news to Evan, but none of them had a happy ending, so she remained silent.

Zoe focused on not looking depressed. She perked up so her sweet husband wouldn't worry and said, "Oh, you know. The usual. The better question is, how was *your* day? You look especially happy tonight."

"Also the usual," he said and paused, clearly for dramatic effect. "At least, until noon." Clearly, he was very excited about something at work.

"Oh, yeah? What happened at noon? It wasn't a gunfight at a corral, was it?" She grinned at him. "I mean, are there even any corrals around here?"

"No, and not that I know of, but a gunfight at a corral also would have been cool. Alas, that was not what happened."

"Do tell. What did occur at noon if not a gunfight, since we don't have any corrals around here? Perhaps we need to look into that one of these days."

Evan gave her a quick hug and a lingering kiss. When he stepped back to stare deeply into her eyes, she almost let her problem slip out. No. He had good news and she refused to ruin it for him. Her issue could wait.

Besides, Zoe loved this man so much it was hard to control herself. Every time she spoke to him even for a little while, she wanted to throw her arms around him, hug him tight and marry him all over again.

He led her into the living room and together they sat down on the sofa. He took her hands in his and Zoe settled her mind to listen to her husband's good news.

"Remember when I told you that I had a friend who got a job at that huge trucking and hauling company that's number one in the state?" Evan asked her.

Zoe squinted. She remembered him talking

about his friends on a regular basis, but didn't recall this particular friend or any trucking and hauling jobs. She shrugged. "No, but go ahead and tell me what happened anyway."

He grinned. "Caleb is one of my good friends from high school in Cape Canaveral Beach. When he graduated from college, he landed a really great job with Henderson Hauling. Did I mention that they are number one in the state?" he asked with a grin.

Zoe laughed. "Cool. Good for him. What did he do at noon?" Zoe was in awe of how many close friends Evan had. Zoe was basically friends with her sister, Evan's sisters, her mother and Evan's mother. Sure, she had friends from high school, but none that she'd stayed as close with as her husband did with his various guy friends.

"Well, when the maintenance department of Henderson Hauling wanted to partner with a hardware store and also a small business owner in the state, Caleb mentioned me and my business to one of the managers. A few weeks back I got a call to inquire if I'd be interested. After almost dropping the phone because I nodded so hard, I managed to say yes! After several more informational calls, a phone interview and three Zoom sessions, they gave me the contract." He looked very happy.

Zoe knew he'd wanted to expand and this was a big win for Evan. "Wow. That's awesome. Does this make you a global businessman now?"

Evan shook his head. "Nothing so daring at

that, but it does make me want to take you out for dinner to celebrate. What do you say?"

"I say, I'm in. Also, I didn't know what we were having for dinner tonight anyway."

"Good thing we need to go out and celebrate, huh?"

"Definitely." Zoe put a smile on her face, trying not to show any concern about her own news. It wasn't that she was unhappy. She was elated for Evan and the boost to his business, but she needed to talk to him about the internship and that wasn't going to happen tonight. They had a celebration to get to and her possible desertion would have to wait until tomorrow.

Perceptive as always, Evan asked her on the way out the door, "Are you okay? You seem a bit quiet and introspective."

Zoe almost blurted out what was on her mind, but those unhappy scenarios from earlier in her brain kept her from saying anything. "I'm fine. Just a long day. I'm grateful we are going out tonight. Thanks for being such an awesome businessman and conquering the world one trucking and hauling company at a time so that I didn't have to figure out what we were going to eat tonight."

He nodded. "I do what I can. Where would you like to go?"

The word Miami came into her mind. Because of course her brain was full of her issue that she needed to discuss, but couldn't talk about yet.

Miami in general made her think of flashy

nightclubs and delicious Cuban food. There was an awesome Cuban place only a few minutes from their home.

"How about Ernesto's?" she asked.

He brightened as if surprised she'd chosen that place, but happy she did. "Excellent choice. Let's go."

Zoe slipped her hand into Evan's, vowing that tomorrow at breakfast, she'd break the news about the internship in Miami. He deserved a night to enjoy his good news. Since she was also a coward, this gave her an out for the evening.

Tomorrow, she vowed. *First thing in the morning,* she vowed again.

Unless, of course, she slept in and missed him before he went to work, because that really did happen sometimes.

The voice inside her head whispered, *Coward.*

∞∞∞

Miranda sat in the waiting room of the lawyer's office, making a mental list of all the things she wanted to say during their appointment. She pulled out a small notepad and made note of a few additional possibly important things she wanted to gripe about. Her largest worry had to do with keeping Bill from getting any part of her Driftwood Inn money or business in a divorce.

The divorce paperwork had been started with a phone call, but obviously hadn't been served to her husband yet. She needed to ensure they expressed her wishes before she signed them.

Miranda wanted to discuss a few more important subjects before letting Bill know her plans. Thus, she was waiting on her scheduled appointment to speak to her new awesome divorce lawyer. Monica Allendale had told her on the phone that she already had someone available who could serve the papers to Bill whenever Miranda was ready.

Bill's possible financial stake in her bed-and-breakfast had become Miranda's primary worry. She'd had a nightmare a few nights ago where Bill took the money from her business and did a whole body reboot. The vision she created in her nightmare had him looking like something horrid and sinister that should be chained up in a basement and never let loose for fear of scaring all the children in the land into a coma.

She didn't even have a basement, but the terrible dream version of Bill had stuck with her into the morning and then all week as she waited for her appointment today.

Miranda really liked this lawyer's office. It was calming. It was not overdecorated. Clearly, this lawyer had her priorities in the right place. She didn't spend billions of dollars on her waiting room. Instead, it was a quiet, serene and lovely space for her possible clients to wait.

One minute before her appointment was set to start, the receptionist called Miranda's name. By the time she was shown into the lawyer's office, her appointment was right on time. The punctuality was another point in her lawyer's favor.

"Hi, Miranda. It's good to see you again," her lawyer said, shaking her hand and gesturing at one of the chairs in front of her desk. "Please, have a seat."

"Thank you so much, Monica," she said. "And thank you also for seeing me last time on such short notice. I'm sure you're very busy. However, I'm unsure of how my husband might react to the divorce. He may be joyful and planning the same thing behind my back, or he might be shocked. I just don't know. Therefore, I wanted to make sure I ironed out all the details first."

"I understand completely, Miranda. Best to have all your ducks in row, so to speak, before you ring the bell and serve him with papers because you can't un-ring that bell no matter what."

"That's the truth. I'm so grateful to my friend Roberta for referring me to you. I know you worked on her daughter's case."

"I can't comment on any other clients or what I did for them, but I do know Roberta Pierce and her daughter, Beth." Monica smiled apologetically, but Miranda understood. Everybody knew she couldn't comment on any other clients; it would be breaking attorney-client privilege.

Her discretion only made Miranda believe

that this lawyer was the best one for her. Clearly, she wasn't a blabbermouth like the family lawyer she and Bill shared. That was good and also a nice change of pace.

"Of course," Miranda said. The phone rang and Monica pushed out a sigh, held up a finger and picked up her phone, but was off in only a few seconds.

"Let's pretend we are meeting for the first time. Tell me everything like I've never heard it before, okay? I find it helps to not only get it all out, but it also can reveal important details." She had a legal pad and pen in hand, ready to take notes.

"Good idea. I think it would help to get it all out. Thanks." Miranda began, "My husband of nearly thirty years has been acting oddly the past several years, like almost a decade, and not in a good way. He's become secretive about his job and he spends way too much money on plastic surgery. He ignores our grown children when he encounters them in public because he doesn't want any of his recent acquaintances to know how old he is.

"But the final straw for me," she said, choosing her words carefully. "Is the fact I caught him at a restaurant with a young woman who looked younger than any of our four children. He is verbally abusive to me on a daily basis. I know this sounds petty and trivial, but he's up every morning hours before I need to wake up, then proceeds to make as much noise as possible in the house. I've asked him repeatedly not to do this, but he ignores me and continues as though he lives alone.

"The lack of sleep in my life, especially recently, isn't helping matters at all. He's not the man I married. He and I have nothing in common anymore. When I asked him what he saw in our future, he said nothing and promptly left the room to stop the conversation. I never thought I would ever say these words in my life, but I want a divorce from my husband."

Monica nodded and continued to write notes. She soon looked up at Miranda and asked, "What about your business? I understand you run a bed-and-breakfast, is that right?"

"Yes. I have for almost fifteen years. What I'm most worried about," Miranda continued, "is my business. I own the Driftwood Inn in Cape Canaveral North. I would like to keep Bill—or rather *William*, as he demands to be called these days—completely out of it during any divorce agreement and splitting of our assets.

"The Inn is in my name solely, which is the way Bill wanted it from the start. I think he was afraid that if I failed, we'd both be bankrupt. But I didn't fail. Therefore, I am the sole proprietor of my business. However, many of our bank accounts are joint accounts. While I do have a business account that was set up quite a number of years ago, I'm afraid that he will have access to it and therefore claim half of my business account money as his. I would like to stop this if I can. Or maybe it won't be a problem, but I don't know."

"Do you file your taxes separately?" she asked.

"We do a joint tax return, but I still have to do up all my income and expenses separately for the business. Our tax accountant separates the bill for the tax preparation as ninety percent going toward my business and ten percent going toward our joint return."

Monica continued to write notes for a solid minute after Miranda stopped talking. When she finally stopped moving her pen, she nodded a couple of times as though she'd worked some things out on her own regarding Miranda's case. She hoped it would be good news and that Bill wouldn't get half of the Driftwood Inn. Most of all, she wished she didn't have to go through this. She had certainly never expected to divorce Bill.

"So as far as your bank accounts are concerned, what you're saying is you have a business account, but not all of your business money is in there?" her lawyer asked.

"The business account was created based on the fact that we already had a joint checking account at the bank. I only operate my money in and out of that account. However, I'm not sure whether they're connected or if Bill has access that I don't know about. I've never tested this theory. Honestly, I never thought I'd have to worry about it, until now."

"First of all, let me officially tell you I'm taking your case. If that wasn't obvious. " She smiled briefly.

"Thank you," Miranda said. She was so relieved. Monica quoted the fee, which was exactly what Miranda had expected. Monica told her to pay the retainer to secure her services at the front desk on her way out, and that would make her officially a client.

"Second of all, I'd like for you to go to your bank as soon as you can and ensure any link between your business account and your husband's access, is severed. If they are separate and you've used them for a decade that way, it shouldn't be a problem. However, it they are connected in some obscure way, you should sever them immediately. Even if you have to transfer your funds and start a brand new account, that would be the best way to ensure you keep what's rightfully yours.

"It may simply require a notification in writing to the bank or extensive paperwork that the bank will need to provide. Unfortunately, it's possible your husband will have to sign something to sever the two accounts if you need to keep your original account for any reason, but don't borrow trouble. Don't mention this matter to him unless it becomes required. Regardless, you need to get started on that right away."

Miranda nodded, planning on heading to the bank the next day.

"You mentioned children earlier. How many still live at home with you?"

"Oh, none of them live with us. All of our

kids are grown and gone. One of my daughters works at the inn occasionally, but she goes to school and has her own home. Eventually she may take the business over for me. At least I hope so."

The lawyer nodded. "Okay. I believe I have all that I need. I'll continue preparing all the paperwork."

"But Bill won't find out what I'm doing quite yet, will he? I don't want him forewarned."

Monica shook her head. "No. I won't file anything until you give me the word. But I'll let you know what the next steps are, and the timeline of any court dates you need to know about when I know them."

"Thank you."

"You're welcome. I'm sorry you have to go through this. I know it's hard, but I'm here to do everything I can to make it as painless as possible. You also need to know that I'm here for you and only you. I'm on *your* side."

"Good. Thanks again." Miranda felt like a boulder rolled right off her shoulders. She was relieved, even as she was struck by a moment of extreme sadness. She missed the Bill she'd married. She wished he had stuck around. But the stranger she was married to was not anyone she wanted to be with, let alone remain married to.

The sooner this was over, the better for everyone involved.

Chapter Thirteen

Zoe woke up the next morning after a wonderful dinner with her husband the night before. They had spent most of the meal discussing his new endeavor with the trucking company, what it would mean for his business and the lift it would give the financial aspect of what Evan had been working so hard to achieve since he opened his hardware store.

Before she looked at the clock, Zoe listened to see if she could hear Evan rustling around in the kitchen. When she didn't hear anything for several seconds, she lifted up from the surface of the bed, intending to basically sneak out. Part of her squirmed that she was such a coward she couldn't tell her husband about the Miami internship.

She swung her legs over the edge of the bed, carefully pushed the rest of the covers away and made her way to the bathroom. When she was done with her morning routine, she stopped at the door to the bedroom, listening again to make sure she was alone. Satisfied that Evan must already be gone, she strolled quietly downstairs to the kitchen.

Rounding the final corner and shooting into the kitchen, she stopped suddenly, almost falling on her face when she saw Evan seated at the breakfast table.

"Whoa! I thought were already gone," Zoe said.

Evan looked up the minute she said the first word, startling in his chair. He'd been hunched over a stack of papers apparently reading quietly, not making any noise and thereby surprising Zoe when she came down to the kitchen believing she was alone.

He gave her a sheepish grin and started scooping papers back into a single pile.

"I've just been going over the paperwork for this new endeavor with the trucking company, making sure I understand all the ins and outs before I sign it." He'd gotten the sheaf of papers into a messy stack.

"And are you going to sign it?" Zoe asked.

"Well, I'm about three quarters of the way through all of the papers and so far I haven't seen anything that doesn't delight me beyond reason." The smile on Evan's face was a sight to behold. Clearly, he was very happy about this new business deal, which of course only made Zoe that much more miserable about having to tell him her news.

Since he was a captive audience, Zoe felt a surge of courage. She straightened and was about to tell him what she should've told him already when Evan looked up at the clock. "Oh no. Is that the right time? I've gotta run or be late for work." He was up out of his chair in a second. He grabbed up the stack of messy papers, shoved them in his bag and was out the door with a brief kiss in her direction before she could even open her mouth.

Zoe turned in time to see the kitchen door close. Shutting her eyes, she lowered her head to face the floor. She was really going to have to make a better effort to tell him what was on her mind. If only she wasn't such a scaredy-cat. She was not afraid of Evan. Heavens, no!

She just didn't want to cause a rift in their relationship so early in their marriage. She should have already told him about the internship. She should have told him what would happen if she accepted the assignment in Miami. She was completely at war with herself about telling him the truth and having him be unhappy about it versus doing a continual dance of joy over the excitement of wanting to get down to Miami and do the best job possible.

Then another thought came into her mind: She was going to have to tell her mother that she would *not* be interning at the Driftwood Inn or the Lighthouse Inn, but would be going to someplace out of town. Someplace more high-rent than the Driftwood Inn or the Lighthouse Inn. Someplace snootier with a much richer clientele than either of the places she thought she would be interning at this summer.

Any way she sliced it, she was going to be

disappointing a few family members. First would be her husband, second would be her mother. After them, she was certain the rest of her family would not be happy that she'd angered the two people she loved the most.

Zoe made herself a cup of coffee, sat at the breakfast table, put a hand beneath her chin and sighed out loud.

Normally, she would call Beverly and confide in her any issue she had, especially if it involved their mother. But this time she wasn't ready to do that. This time she was afraid her sister would side with their mother and maybe she would be right to do so. On top of everything else, both her mother and sister were having marital issues and she didn't want to be yet another problem piled on their already burdened lives.

She entertained a brief thought about calling one of her twin brothers for a serious conversation about her life choices, but while she loved them both beyond reason, they were not talkative about feelings or relationships on a good day. And putting them in the position of choosing between her and their mother was a losing proposition from the get-go. She dismissed the idea immediately.

Zoe had never felt so alone. Did she really want to go to Miami? Was it even an option to turn down the internship? The answer was yes and no.

Therefore, she needed to suck it up and make things happen. Once she gave her final yes to the internship, it would be off to the races. She only had a couple of months before she was going to have to take off, leave the city and set up a new temporary home in a fancy hotel well south of where she lived.

When she was in Miami, it was likely she would again be all alone and have a lot of family members angry at her. No wonder she was putting a decision off.

The thought of hurting her husband or any member of her family made her physically sick. She took a sip of coffee and decided it was time to shake off this stupid melancholy. It was time to go forth and tell the truth and let the chips fall where they may.

Evan always told her during the rare times they argued that he couldn't fix the problem if he didn't know what the problem was. She hated to burst his bubble when he was so happy about his new business opportunity, but this problem was truly weighing her down. He was going to figure out she was miserable and stressed anyway if she kept this to herself much longer.

Besides, Evan was her very best friend. Her mother and Beverly tied for second place in that arena. So Zoe vowed to tell Evan about this *today*. And she would also tell her mother *today*.

Zoe kicked aside the cowardly voice that tried to persuade her to keep quiet until the last possible second. She downed the rest of her coffee in one long swig and headed upstairs to get dressed and make a surprise visit to her husband's hardware store.

∞ ∞ ∞

After being rudely interrupted at lunch, William had dropped Kaylee off at the clinic, drove back to the bank and sat in the parking lot thinking about his future. He was so angry at his wife.

Miranda had no right! No right at all! To tell Kaylee how old he was in public like that. It was a bridge too far. It was uncalled for. He wasn't sure what to do with all the anger that ricocheted through his body right now. He fairly vibrated with fury.

He glanced at the clock on his dashboard and realized he was late getting back. He shrugged mentally. What difference did it make? Every day he went to work was like a lie he had to keep buried deep inside. He hated working at the bank more than anything.

About ten years ago, he'd been on top of the world. He had been the senior loan officer. He had an office to himself, a nice, quiet, private office, and a private receptionist to take his calls, schedule his appointments and make his life easier.

Then, a few years ago, a new partner was brought on board at the bank.

The person was a silent partner and therefore no one at the bank, at least none of the regular staff, knew who it was. But William found out, because the man was an idiot and made William's life difficult forever after.

Once the new partner was fully brought on board and had his silent little fingers in the bank's business, he started making some changes. The first several changes had to do with the general staff and nothing to do with William, so he didn't care. As long as everyone left him alone to do his work the way he wanted to do his work, he was fine.

That didn't last for long.

The silent partner decided William no longer needed to be a senior account manager or a senior loan officer or a senior anything. In one fell swoop, William lost his prestigious private office, his private receptionist that catered only to him and, worst of all, they reduced his pay by fifteen percent.

The bank president, Theodore Harkin, had seemed sincerely sorry that these changes needed to be taken, but told William it was necessary for the health of the bank and its future. That was when William decided to find out who this foolish silent partner was and give that person a piece of his mind.

It took William almost a year to figure it out. He settled in at his new desk in the middle of the bank like he was some common person, but he wasn't. He plastered a smile on his face and pretended like the demotion and pay cut was no big deal. Like he'd practically been about to ask for this very thing, to be a nobody sitting in the middle of the bank at a substandard desk, making less money than he always had.

He spent all that year working out a way to find out the identity of the silent partner. It hadn't been easy. Every time he thought he was about to find out, he'd been thwarted. But that just made him try even harder.

After failing so many times trying to do things the legal way, he had gone a slightly illegal way, paying someone to find out for him. And when the loan shark he'd hired to find out had told him that Jeremiah Peyton was the bank's new silent partner, William got furious all over again.

The identity of the silent partner who'd ruined his life was vile. The very name Peyton made his blood boil. The Peytons were a well-established family in Cape Canaveral North. They had been one of the founding families of the town. They'd been here long enough to build up quite the reputation for being hard in business, hard in the community and hard pretty much to everybody who wasn't as rich as they were. And there were very few people who had as much money as the Peytons.

Jeremiah Peyton, patriarch of the Peyton family, was the silent partner who had come into the place where William had worked for decades and promptly ruined his life.

William would never forgive Peyton for the humiliation of how he'd been treated at the establishment where he'd worked for over two decades. No matter what. He didn't care. Not going to happen. The man was dead to him.

As soon as William found out, not exactly legally, about Jeremiah Peyton's silent partnership with his employer, William made an appointment to see Mr. Peyton at his other business. The overt business where he was *not* a silent partner, but basically shouted it to the world that he was the richest financier in the county. Maybe even the state. Who knew? William didn't know and he didn't care.

The meeting had not gone according to what William had planned. Admittedly, he had been very riled up by the time he got to the meeting with Peyton. He'd stormed in and expected the man to apologize for ruining William and changing his life in such a dramatic way.

William felt like he was justified in his anger and didn't stop to think about the consequences of not only what he said but his actions while in Mr. Peyton's posh, luxurious office.

"I know for a fact you're the silent partner the First Bank of Canaveral in Cape Canaveral North." That was the first thing William said when he was shown into the office by Peyton's beautiful assistant. Once she'd closed the door, leaving the two men alone, William let loose. He didn't cross his arms but stood six feet from the edge of Peyton's desk, hands fisting at his sides, waiting for the man to understand why he was there and what he was about.

Jeremiah Peyton hadn't so much as lifted in eyebrow in his direction. In a completely rude and insulting manner, the man had continued reading and typing on his computer as if William didn't even exist and didn't have an appointment with him.

William watched him and his anger grew and grew. After what seemed like an hour but was probably only three to five minutes, William asked, "Well? Aren't you going to say anything?"

Peyton had looked up from his work and given William a snide smile, and that really made his blood boil. "I don't know what you want. You come in here and accuse me of something that even you aren't sure is true. I really don't know what you expect me to do. Do you want me to bow and scrape to you because you've found something out—illegally, would be my guess—that is absolutely none of your business?" Jeremiah Peyton then stood up. "Well, I won't."

William was taken aback. He was the wronged person here, not Peyton. Why did the man insist on not doing what was expected? He had an epiphany right then. However, before he could adjust his attitude, because he'd really played this whole meeting all wrong, Peyton shoved his desk chair backward, letting it crash against the wall, and walked around his enormous and expensively carved desk. He marched across the thick, plush, incredibly expensive carpet until he was nose to nose with William.

"I know who you are, Mr. William Cole, and let me be the first to tell you that I'm not at all impressed. Not even the tiniest little bit. If I were a silent partner in the bank where you work, and I'm not saying I am, any businessman with half a brain would look at all the financials and assess where best to cut the fat and waste out of any business."

William, still trying to catch up to the conversation, said, "I'm not fat or wasteful." He should've kept his mouth shut. But the man egged him on with every look, word and facial expression. His very presence made William say stupid things he didn't mean to say. How could he gain the upper hand here?

Peyton frowned. "Well, your opinion is self-serving and wrong." Peyton then took a half step back, chuckling as if William were nothing, no one and not worthy of any attention. "If I were a silent partner in the bank where you work, and again I'm not saying that I am, I would've probably fired you for being so useless. However, since any silent partner would not have complete autonomy over any business, that silent partner might have been overruled when he wanted to cut the obvious blubber and waste out of the business." He shook his head and looked at William like he was a fool, like he was of no concern, like he was a loser. Peyton turned on his heel and headed back to his desk, as if William were no more important than a fly he wanted to swat away from his person.

"I am not through with you," William said. "I demand to have my old job back and my private office and my receptionist and my former income level."

"Or else what?" Peyton had arrived at the side of his desk and half-turned to ask his question.

William stared at him. He didn't have an *or else*. Why hadn't he thought this through better? He thought back to big Eddie V, wondering if the loan shark had any more information on Jeremiah Peyton that he could use against the man. Again he thought, *I should've thought this through better and had an* or else *to offer up. Next time I'll be better prepared.*

He straightened, adjusted his tie and said, "This isn't over, Peyton. Wait and see."

Peyton said, "You're wrong, Cole. This *is* over. I never want to see you again. You're lucky I even allowed you to make this meeting in the first place. Trust me, the next time you call there will never be a meeting available to the likes of you. Just carry your blubber back to your desk and be grateful you even have a job, you sniveling coward."

William really wanted to punch Peyton in the face, but he needed his job. Plus, he wasn't really supposed to be here because he shouldn't know who the silent partner was. Peyton hadn't boldly admitted to being the silent partner, but William knew he was. Since he wasn't supposed to know, he didn't want to have to explain how he knew or who he'd paid to get the information.

Big Eddie V, the local loan shark in Cape Canaveral Beach, had smiled with satisfaction when he told William who the silent partner was. William thought at the time that Big Eddie V knew more about the silent partner, Jeremiah Peyton, then he let on. But if William wanted more information, he'd have to pay more for it and at the time he didn't want to. He should have. He should've gotten every single piece of information possible on Jeremiah Peyton before he stormed into the man's office.

Peyton had a smug look on his fat face. William did the only thing he could. He gave Peyton his best look of disdain, turned on his heel and left. Fury coursed through his veins as he exited the man's office, then the building and stomped into the parking garage.

William was so angry he barely knew how to control himself. He was so angry that he drove himself back to work without remembering exactly how he'd gotten there. Once he was parked in his personal space at the bank, the very last perk he was allowed to keep, he vowed to do whatever he could to foil the Peytons in the future.

No matter how small of an incident, he would not give an inch in their direction. Ever!

He briefly thought of how his eldest daughter had disgraced herself by marrying Noah Peyton, Jeremiah Peyton's only son. He had refused to walk Beverly down the aisle until he found out she was pregnant. It was all he could do not to stamp his feet and shake her at the mere thought of mixing his blood with those horrible people. However, his daughter having the bastard child of one of the Peytons seemed worse. So he had agreed to walk her down the aisle, grimacing the entire time. He hated that whole day.

The worst part was finding out his daughter had lost the baby a week before the wedding. He would never forgive her for that disgrace. Never!

William pushed out a long sigh, unhappy with the way his life was going right now. Here he was, years later, again sitting in the parking lot outside the bank where he worked, fuming over something he couldn't take back. But this time it wasn't Peyton who had angered him. Instead, he was furious at his wife, Miranda. She had absolutely no right to do what she'd done. Sneaking up on him while he was having a perfectly innocent lunch with a friend and making a scene.

And she had the audacity to tell Kaylee how old he was, threatening her as if Kaylee wasn't just the sweetest girl he'd ever known. William knew he needed to get back to work, but he was too angry. He sat in his car for nearly twenty minutes before he calmed down enough to exit his car and go inside.

He walked into the bank where he'd spent

nearly thirty years of his life working, for all the good it had done him. He was only a few steps higher than he'd been when he started.

However, when he passed the loan officer's desk, he noticed a sign that had been put up like a vertical banner. It said, "Ask me how you can afford your next luxury vacation in California."

The picture on the advertisement had an ocean and a house on the beach and looked like the perfect place to live. He stared at the picture, trying to imagine what it would be like to live on the other side of the country. William did live on the beach, but the house in the picture looked so much nicer than the ramshackle place he shared with Miranda.

California. Interesting. And just like that, a brand new and marvelous idea popped into his head.

This new idea made him very happy. It made him so delighted that he spent another twenty minutes thinking about what he'd have to do to make this new idea a reality.

He was supposed to be cataloguing boring files regarding the lockboxes in the vault. Instead of doing that, he thought about California. The new idea started to take shape. The new idea was genius. He was going to be smart about this. Instead of running into the fray without thinking everything through, this time William was going to plan. He was going to go step-by-step in order to realize this very great idea and make it happen.

When he continued walking to his own desk, it was the first time he'd felt happy going into work in years. But he would need this job for just a little while longer and then he would kiss it good-bye without a single regret.

William thought about confronting Miranda with his genius new idea but decided no, he would not tell her. She'd only be angry and he didn't need that crap in his life. He never needed crap from Miranda ever again. He fairly skipped to his desk with a smile on his face and a happy dance in his step.

He couldn't wait to tell Kaylee about his new genius idea. He was certain she would also be very happy. Had she ever been to California? Did she want to go? What was he thinking, of course she'd want to go. Why wouldn't she?

Chapter Fourteen

Miranda had a meeting with Theo Jackson in his construction office. She had hoped to see Nathan around somewhere, but Lucy, the sweet girl who was Theo's receptionist, told her he was at a job site across town, finishing up the last construction job so that they could start her expansion project on Monday morning.

She nodded, not too disappointed. She was very anxious to see her son on a regular basis at the worksite of her new addition to the Driftwood Inn. Lucy asked, "Are you excited to get this started? I know you've been wanting this done for a while and you had to wait for Theo's schedule to open up."

"I am very excited. And I didn't mind waiting. I just really hope he can get it done in time for my annual Christmas party." Miranda brightened. "And of course you'll be invited to the Christmas party, too."

Lucy grinned. "Really?" She was very cute. Miranda wondered if she was single. "

All of a sudden, Miranda had a great idea. Maybe while Lucy was at the party, Miranda would make sure she was introduced to Gabe.

Nathan had told her repeatedly that he might never get married or have children. He hadn't said it in a while, but she figured he still felt that way.

Gabe, on the other hand, was a viable match-making option. Maybe Miranda would work on setting Lucy up with Gabe well before the annual Christmas party. She made a mental note to think up a way to get them together.

"Of course. The whole crew will be invited. It's an annual tradition and while I've always managed to do it in the kitchen and ground floor areas at the Driftwood Inn, I would love to christen the new addition by having my fifteenth annual Christmas party in it. I even designed a special room just for that purpose."

"Well, then, I'll do everything within my power to make sure that it's done and I look forward to attending the party, even though it's eight months away."

Just then, Theo opened the door and came into the construction office. He smiled as soon as he saw Miranda and said, "Hey, Mrs. Cole. How are you doing this morning?"

"I'm doing very well, thank you for asking." Miranda stood up as he approached. He extended a hand, which she shook, and escorted her down a short hallway to his office.

Once seated before his desk, Miranda handed him an envelope with the check for one third of the cost of the renovation. He took the envelope from her and laid it on his desk without opening it to look at it. She thought it was sweet that he trusted her enough not to even take a peek, taking it for granted that it was the exact amount they had discussed.

And it was.

"We are all set to begin on Monday. My crew is cleaning up the last work to be done at another jobsite. As matter of fact, that's where Nathan is, in case you wondered."

"That's what your receptionist Lucy told me."

"With this down payment," he put his finger on the envelope, "I'll be able to buy all the materials I need to get started. And then your next payment won't be due until three months from now. Will that be okay?"

"That will be perfectly fine." She opened her purse and pulled out her pocket calendar, noting the date three months from now when she'd have to pay the second installment. She would do the same thing she had this time—go to the bank and get a cashier's check for the amount.

"The second payment will be the exact same as this payment." He tapped the closed envelope again and added, "but then the final payment will be plus or minus this amount because of things I don't know about yet." He smiled. "But it won't be too far off either way, okay?"

"I understand."

"And I promise you that it won't be a big surprise. I'll make sure you know exactly how much is accumulating as we go along after the second payment. If you want, we can meet once a month those final three months and I can keep you apprised of the running tab."

"I appreciate that, Theo. And I'm grateful you don't need the whole amount up front."

Theo waved a hand in front of his face as if that was no problem and stood up to shake her hand. "I'm anxious to get started on this project and I know that you really want to open in time for your annual Christmas party. I will do everything in my power to make that happen."

"I know you will," Miranda said. "And I'm really excited to get started."

"And also because I love that annual party and really want to attend in the new place." He grinned.

"Well, even if it's delayed, your whole crew will be invited no matter where we hold it."

"My guys will like that a lot." Getting back to business, he said, "So, the noise level shouldn't be too bad in the first month or so. We'll mostly be digging and building forms to set the foundation. The loud stuff comes when we start hammering nails to build the structure and also when we build the inside rooms, put up the sheetrock and the like."

"That's okay," Miranda said. "By then it will be the off-season and I won't be as crowded as I usually am in the summer months. And if anyone insists on wanting to rent a room on that side of the inn, I'll tell them up front about the possible noise."

"Good enough. It's a pleasure doing business with you, Mrs. Cole."

"Thank you so much, Theo. I know you're going to do a great job."

Miranda let Theo walk her to the construction office door. She waved at Lucy on her way by and exited with a happy step. If she were younger, she might have leapt in the air and clicked her heels together. But she did smile and send up wishes for a speedy yet safe construction project. Even though she was now committed to a very large and expensive renovation project, Miranda was so excited she could hardly hold herself together and not dance to her car. She couldn't wait until it was all done.

Even though her marriage was falling apart, her business life was soaring. Miranda thought about Bill. A sudden feeling like she needed to make one more effort to straighten things out between them arose.

Yes, she'd already seen a divorce lawyer. Yes, she had already started the paperwork for a divorce. Even so, she felt like a nearly thirty-year marriage deserved one more chance to rekindle. The harsh reality was she didn't have any hopes that they could reconcile unless he was willing to make some major changes.

Still, Miranda felt obligated to give it one last chance. She drove by the bank where Bill worked, but didn't see his car in the parking lot. She glanced at her watch and noted that it was close to lunch time. Perhaps he was out eating. She could only hope that he was alone, although she suspected he was not. Her anger level rose up, but she tried to take a deep breath and calm herself. The air only helped a little.

Miranda decided she would talk to Bill tonight after dinner. Or perhaps she would try to catch him at work after lunch. She could call him and invite him to a special dinner for just the two of them in the kitchen at the inn.

She had a few more errands to run today, and she needed to go relieve Darby at the front desk so she could go to lunch. The more she thought about it, the more Miranda realized that she wouldn't feel right about things if she didn't give it one more try. One more discussion to see if they could salvage their relationship. Almost thirty years was a really long time to just throw away without giving it a try one last time.

Miranda drove past a stretch of businesses in a strip mall, along one side of the street, where there was only a sidewalk and no parking. Or perhaps the parking was behind the building, she wasn't certain.

What Miranda could see clearly was her husband of almost thirty years in a bear hug with the young woman she'd seen him with the other day at lunch. They were kissing.

Kissing!

It was quite shocking to see her husband kissing someone else. Out in public. Right outside and in the light of day where everybody and anybody could see them, including her. It was a good thing there were no other cars driving nearby or she might have slammed into one of them.

Miranda was so jolted and appalled by the public display of affection between her husband and a girl young enough to be their daughter that she nearly drove into the curb a few yards from them. She wheeled her car away just in time and kept going, wondering if she'd just dreamt what she'd seen. No. That vision of him with his Elvis hair, plastic face and his lips pressed to that girl's mouth was going to be burned into her brain forevermore.

She was so stunned by what she'd witnessed that she drove all the way back to the Driftwood Inn and parked in her spot without really remembering how she got there. She probably looked ridiculous, but she just sat in her car staring at nothing, thinking about what she'd just seen. The vision slammed into her brain over and over and over again. If she hadn't seen it with her own two eyes she might not have believed it.

However, it did relieve her of one burden she'd been unsure of all day. There was one thing she did not have to do.

Miranda, who had been about to give Bill a

second chance, decided quickly that Bill didn't deserve any more chances. She was done. She was really well and truly done with her husband forever.

∞ ∞ ∞

Beverly had truly outdone herself at breakfast with regard to her husband and poking the bear, as it were. An older couple had been seated next to them maybe eight feet away at about the same time the waiter brought their breakfast to them.

She had been about to wave at the older couple, which was akin to social suicide, according to the Peytons. People waved at *them* first, not the other way around. Ever.

But she noticed the waiter moving in their direction and quelled the urge to wave at the strangers like a hayseed with a big grin on her face like it was her first time in the big city. She was really having fun.

The waiter put her plate down in front of her. Half the plate was covered with the crispiest looking hash browns she'd ever seen. She looked up at her husband to see his reaction.

Noah sneered at her. Sneered. He also shook his head as if supremely disappointed in her clearly vulgar choices.

Beverly mentally shrugged because she was also fairly disappointed in her choice of a husband. She figured they were equal as it stood.

She picked up her fork and cut into the delicious hash browns first. They were crispy on the outside and soft in the middle. Perfect. The first bite she took, an unexpected moan escaped her lips.

Even though she had been planning to do that very thing on purpose, the hash browns tasted so good she moaned without even trying. Beverly opened her eyes in time to see her husband's reaction to the unexpected noise.

Noah gave her a look she'd never seen before. The look that said, "If I could kill you with my bare hands right now I would. However, there are witnesses, so I won't." His frown was so ferocious she expected him to start screaming and ranting and doing all manner of improper things at the country club breakfast table. She was unimpressed by his attitude.

Beverly swallowed her first delectable bite of hash browns and then gave him a very wide grin. "These are the most delicious hash browns I've ever eaten," she said, allowing a dreamy tone to slip into her voice. One she knew would really push him over the edge.

The woman at the table eight feet away turned her head and smiled, as if in approval of Beverly's reaction to her hash browns. She smiled back and sent the woman a finger wave.

Noah looked like he was about to have a major heart attack as he sat like a statue across from her, breathing in and out so hard and heavy she thought maybe he was going to take flight or blow her house down. She figured it was Peyton family approved, because the woman smiled first, but Noah clearly wasn't paying attention to the standard family rules. They did have a way of changing just when Beverly thought she'd figured them out. Either way, she didn't care. Her attitude right now was *in for a penny, in for a pound.*

Beverly pretended she couldn't even see her foolish husband, because he was so completely ridiculous. If he wanted to have an attack over her being friendly and enjoying her food, so be it.

She found it was freeing not to worry about what Noah thought. It was so much nicer to enjoy a meal without constantly worrying that every syllable she uttered and every morsel that entered her mouth was the worst mistake she'd ever made in her life. It was so wonderful not to be under the strictest of scrutiny, while others were ready to pounce on her for every tiny mistake they thought she had made.

She suddenly realized she hadn't really made any mistakes. The Peytons just went out of their way to criticize her no matter what she did or said. Beverly faced a lifetime of this attitude from Noah's family. Did she want that? No. She really did not.

She didn't think it had been a mistake to

agree to marry Noah when she thought she was pregnant. Noah had been so sweet to marry her after she'd lost the baby. That was what kept her trying all this time to keep their marriage together.

However, after spending time with his family, she realized he was just like they were. He may have had a short rebellious period while he was dating her, but he sure went straight back to his pompous ways not long after they were married.

Why he'd bothered to marry her if he was only going the turn into a pompous member of his family anyway, she didn't know. Had he thought she was some sort of special social project that he needed to conquer and bend to his will? Had he thought he could change her into a rich put-upon robot like the rest of his family all acted like they were? She wasn't sure. What she did know was that a sense of freedom filled her. The feeling she'd long thought had been destroyed.

Beverly was free. In this moment, she was flying high. She was going to enjoy every second of Noah's discomfort and displeasure.

She would certainly have to pay the price for it tonight when he got home. Beverly wasn't even certain what the price was going to end up being. Once the emotional bill for this breakfast had been handed to her by her pompous and ridiculous husband, she wondered if she would be able to pay it. Or if she would just snatch it out of his hand, rip it in half and walk away, laughing.

The idea of walking away from her husband,

and her home with him, filled her with such a beacon of hope and light she wondered why she'd never seriously thought of it before. Was there anything at her home that she wanted to take with her if, or rather when, she left?

There were a couple of sentimental things that her family had given her that she wanted to make sure she got back. If she had to leave everything Noah had ever bought her behind in that home, it would be worth it. She wouldn't miss anything, starting with this stupid, too expensive yellow party dress she was wearing for breakfast at the club. It, too, was truly ridiculous. The woman eight feet away was wearing a similar style of dress that Beverly had changed out of this morning, which just confirmed to her she'd been dressed just fine. Noah just didn't want to deal with her.

How did that *work out for you, Mister Pompous?* she thought.

Beverly hoped she would be free, because the worst thing Noah could do to her now was insist she stay and work things out.

Chapter Fifteen

Miranda snapped out of her mental anguish, dug through her purse for the business card for her lawyer and retrieved her cell phone. She dialed the number, which she was quickly beginning to memorize, and was surprised when Monica herself answered.

"Monica?" Miranda asked. "Did I dial your private number instead of your office number? I'm so sorry, I'm just planning to leave a message with your receptionist."

"You got the right number," Monica said. "My receptionist had a minor family emergency, so I had to start answering my own phones." She laughed. "I find it does me good. What can I do for you, Miranda? You sound upset."

"Yes. I am very upset. I just saw my husband kissing another woman out in public for all the world to see. I'm in shock and I just can't believe it." After telling her lawyer what she'd seen, Miranda sat quietly staring out her window, still in disbelief.

"Oh, Miranda, I'm so very sorry. This is hard enough without visuals burned into your mind.

What would you like me to do?"

Miranda didn't answer for a few seconds as she gathered her thoughts. Finally, she said, "I was about to give him a second chance, but not anymore. I want to proceed with the divorce as soon as possible. When is the soonest he can be served with divorce papers?"

"It can be within the next week or two, but I'd like to ensure that your bank accounts are severed before I do. Have you been able to straighten it out with your bank?"

Miranda sighed. "I have an appointment in two days with the bank officer who can help me. He was not available sooner, unfortunately."

"I'll tell you what I'll do. I'll get everything ready. All you'll need to do is come in and sign it and you can do it whenever you want. My receptionist is a notary, so she can officiate the paperwork as soon as you sign it. However, if you run into some sort of problem at your bank, we can postpone the delivery to a later date. I already have somebody in mind who can serve your husband the papers whenever it is the right time to do so."

"Thank you, Monica. I appreciate your help. I will go to the bank tomorrow morning and see if I can get an earlier appointment. Maybe I'll just sit at his desk until he shows up."

Monica laughed. "Good for you. Meanwhile, I will continue as though we are serving him the divorce papers in one week unless you tell me to slow my roll, because you need time to sever your bank accounts, which I will."

It was Miranda's turn to laugh at Monica's "slow my roll" comment. It was the first time she'd cracked a smile since she almost drove into a curb after seeing Bill kissing that woman.

Miranda said, "Thanks again." Her lawyer also said goodbye and then hung up.

She likely looked ridiculous just sitting in her car in the parking lot of the bed-and-breakfast she owned. Miranda didn't care. She needed a minute. She might need several minutes.

She pondered the idea of whether to tell her children what she was doing before the papers were served. She quickly decided against it, even though she was fairly certain all of her children would side with her. She didn't want to find out otherwise at this point or put them the awkward position of keeping one parent's secret from the other parent.

∞∞∞

Beverly spent the day out and about shopping, spending money on the credit cards she was certain would be cancelled at any time. So far, they hadn't been rejected.

She bought what she considered practical things. Things she might need if she was starting over from scratch all on her lonesome. Would she be able to move back in with her parents? She sure hoped so. She suspected her mother was in much the same boat as she was as far as marital concerns.

Beverly did not want to intrude on her parents' breakup. Besides, her father still wasn't speaking to her after two-plus years of marriage to a Peyton. She didn't know why, but her father loathed the Peyton family. She thought it had something to do with Noah's father.

It was why he had stopped speaking to her when she married Noah. Before the wedding, when she had admitted she was marrying Noah Peyton because she was pregnant, her father had been particularly aggrieved. She'd never told anyone what he'd said, but her father had called Noah the demon spawn of his worst enemy.

Clearly he had some issue with Noah's father. Beverly didn't disagree that the Peytons were awful, especially now that she'd spent some quality time with all of them and learned so much more than she'd known before about snooty and snobby folks.

Admittedly, if Beverly went home tonight and Noah kicked her out, then it would be a good idea to have a place to go. She didn't want to move in with Zoe and Evan because they were newlyweds. And she refused to move in with her two brothers, who had an apartment about the size of a shoebox. Not to mention the fact that it was crowded and was never as clean as she thought it should be. And she wasn't even picky.

The only place she really had to go was her parents' house. To that end, she took all of her purchases and dropped the packages off at the cottage she'd grown up in. No one was there, of course, because her mother worked across the parking lot at the Driftwood Inn and her father went to his job at a bank in town every day. She didn't know what he did nor did she care. If she moved in, she wouldn't have to talk to him because he refused to talk to her.

While her father may have been right about Noah and his family, he was just one more ridiculous male figure in her life. He'd gone overboard trying to lift, stretch and smooth his face into being thirty again. Well, he wasn't thirty and he just looked like a caricature of the father she'd loved so much growing up.

The fit he'd had when she married Noah may have been warranted, but she took issue with the fact that he treated her like trash after he found out she'd lost the baby that had prompted her semi-shotgun wedding in the first place. For the past couple of years, he'd not spoken to her. Not a word. It was like she was Amish and he had shunned her, pretending like he couldn't see her and wouldn't speak to her even if she stood next to him.

Not too long ago, she had been with Zoe in town when they ran into him coming out of a store meant for men younger than he was. She did her best to be civil, but he didn't look at her or speak to her, even when Zoe said, "Dad, don't be mean. Beverly's right here. Talk to her."

"Beverly?" Their father had said, looking into the air as if trying to recall someone in his life named Beverly but couldn't quite place her. "I don't know anyone with that name."

"Dad," Zoe had tried again. "She's right here." Zoe had pointed at Beverly, but their father was not going to budge.

"So sorry. I've got to run. Bye, Zoe." He'd kissed the air near Zoe's face and walked off without uttering a word to Beverly. He hadn't even looked in her direction during the whole incident.

As far as men who were still speaking to her, Beverly was down to only her younger brothers. She knew the twins also thought their father was acting like a poop-head. She'd heard he also didn't talk to his children when he was with work clients, because apparently he didn't want anyone to think he was old enough to have children in their mid- to late twenties.

Beverly knocked on her parents' door to ensure no one was home. She then used the spare key hidden in a rock by the flowerbed on the right-hand side, went inside and dropped her packages off in the spare guest bedroom, the room she used to share with Zoe growing up.

She'd be sure to mention the package drop-off to her mother.

In the club dining room, after she'd moaned over every single bite of the truly spectacular hash browns, she slowly ate the eggs Benedict and fruit as if she didn't have a care in the world.

Noah ate his breakfast, stabbing and cutting it as if his breakfast had done something awful to him personally. The couple nearby had glanced at them a few times during their stilted meal, but Zoe only smiled.

Once Noah was finished with the violent consumption of his food, he picked up his paper, stood without speaking a word to her and exited, leaving her there like discarded trash.

It was quite a statement, for a prestigious Peyton family club member to get up and leave his wife there and not escort her out. But that was his problem, not hers.

There would likely be a call out to the family and every single Peyton in the county proper would be notified that there had been a public spat between her and Noah at the club.

Beverly was certain that the first question asked would be, "What did Beverly do now? Thank someone for pouring water again? How pedestrian of her."

Beverly didn't care.

She glanced at her watch as she re-hid the key to her parents' house and texted her mom about her purchases in the spare room, so she wouldn't forget to tell her.

Beverly hopped back in her car and headed for the grocery store. She needed a few things to make dinner, pretending like things were normal.

If Noah could pretend to be an entitled snob, she could pretend that things were hunky dory and continue on like she hadn't made Noah, hostile over breakfast this morning.

In fact, Beverly planned to make something very special. What *that* meant was, really expensive.

On her grocery list for this evening's meal were two large T-Bone steaks, two lobsters, baked potatoes—Noah would hate that—Caesar salad items, several varieties of the most expensive imported cheese available, some Italian green olives and the most expensive crackers she could find to make a charcuterie tray for an appetizer.

Pondering what she'd have time to make for dessert, Beverly decided baked Alaska was probably too time restrictive. She'd buy the most expensive cake or pie or whatever was available at the store bakery.

If she'd thought of it, Beverly would have gone to Evan's sister's place, Cake Canaveral Bakery in Cape Canaveral Beach. She loved what Emily had named her shop, and Emily made some very delicious cakes. Alas, she wouldn't have time to drive there without her groceries wilting in the heat. Next time.

There was a sudden rap on her window, making her jump and drop her list. She turned to the side and saw a guy dressed in some sort of uniform with grease and dirt smeared over his shirt, like from a garage. She looked at this hat. It said,

Canaveral Tow Service.

What?

The grease-stained man gestured for her to roll down her window. She didn't want to, but lowered it a crack.

"What do you want?" she said, using her frightened rich woman voice.

"I'm supposed to tow this car."

"What? Who told you to tow it?"

"Mr. Noah Peyton." He didn't even need to consult a piece of paper or a receipt or anything. He knew exactly who'd sent him. Anyone with the last name of Peyton commanded automatic respect or possibly fear or some combination of both things.

"That's my husband," she said through the crack. "Why would he want to tow my car away?" But as she said the words out loud to the tow operator with the grease-stained shirt, she knew exactly why.

"I don't know who you are, lady. And I don't care. All I know is that I need to tow this car pronto. So you need to get out of it. Pronto." The man gave her a look that said he planned to tow her car whether she got out or not.

Beverly held up a forefinger and reached for her cellphone. She did not expect Noah to do anything this public, but perhaps he'd gotten special dispensation from his family to make a scene since they all thought she was such a disaster.

Even so, before she surrendered her vehicle, Beverly speed-dialed her husband on her cell phone to ensure he knew how unhappy she was about this scenario. She was expecting him to avoid her call and let it go to voicemail, where she planned to use every foul four-letter word she knew to tell him exactly how she felt about this debacle.

To her surprise, he answered. "What?"

"Noah, why are you having my car towed?"

He laughed, using his evil tone. "You know exactly why."

"Do I? I mean, I'm here at the grocery store. I was about to pick up steaks for dinner. How can I make dinner if I don't have a car?"

"Did you think your stunt at breakfast would go unanswered?"

"I'm sure I don't know what you mean, Noah. I thought breakfast was lovely."

"Well, Beverly, I'm eating at the club with my family tonight so I don't care about your previous plans or really what happens to you ever again." She heard a quiet click on the other end of the line as he hung up the phone.

The tow guy had heard everything that Noah said because her phone had automatically connected the call to her car's premium audio system. He rapped on her window once more. "Let's go, lady. I haven't got all day."

Beverly wanted to say, "Well, too bad. Apparently I've got the rest of my life to just sit here and think about what I've done."

Anger rose up inside like it had earlier in the day when Noah had abandoned her after making her change clothes. This time, she didn't seek revenge. This time she calmly and carefully retrieved her purse from the passenger seat, adjusted her sunglasses using the cosmetic mirror in her sun visor and pushed the button start to turn the car off. The air conditioner ceased circulating, and the interior warmed up quickly.

She left the window cracked and slowly exited the car, pretending she was a queen and was tossing this unacceptable vehicle to the side. She left the door open and walked away.

The guy called after her, saying she was supposed to leave the key fob, but she pretended not to hear him. Noah could get the car re-keyed, rendering the key fob in her purse useless. But it felt good to hang on to it in this situation.

Beverly didn't know what she was going to do beyond stroll around the grocery store in their nice chilly air conditioning until something useful occurred to her.

Even though she was probably homeless as well as vehicle-less, Beverly didn't care. She was essentially free. Now that she knew Noah was going to be at the club with his family tonight, she wondered if perhaps she should get a taxi and head back to the house to grab whatever she could that she wanted to keep. She glanced at her watch and made a plan to do just that later tonight. Perhaps she could enlist her sister or both of her brothers to help her while Noah was at the club with his family not caring anything about her anymore.

Noah might call the police on her and have her arrested for theft. She did have a driver's license with her home address on it, so maybe the police would cut her some slack.

The only things she wanted from that house were a few personal items her family had given her. She did not plan to keep anything Noah had given her. On second thought, she should grab the jewelry box in case she needed money. She could hock some of the trinkets Noah had given her. And she'd be sure to call him and tell him what she'd done because it would make him mad and make his family even more hostile. She didn't care what Noah's family thought about her anymore.

There would be no more stink-eye looks from the Peyton family. There would be no more feeling like the poo-poo in the punch bowl of their rich, mostly useless put-upon lives. And there would be no more country club meals with Noah's family rolling their eyes at her, making note of every single thing they thought she did wrong.

Like using the words "thank you" too often to the servants and lesser people.

Beverly was probably in shock, with the whole confrontation with the tow-truck guy in the parking lot of the grocery store, when she hadn't even planned to go there until after leaving her mother's house. Wait a minute. Beverly stopped in the frozen foods section, staring at the aisle eleven sign above it, thinking furiously about the tow-truck incident.

How did Noah know where she was going to be when she didn't even know she was going there until she'd left her parents' place? Had he put a GPS tracker on her car?

Chapter Sixteen

Zoe took her time getting ready to go see Evan at work. What that meant was she lollygagged and went as slowly as possible. She spent way too much time getting ready, picking out something to wear and getting herself out the door and into her car.

Once she started her car and just sat there, Zoe rolled her eyes at herself and picked up the pace. It was going to be fine. She hoped.

She drove to the Cape Canaveral Hardware store, found a parking space close to the entrance, pulled in and put the car into park. She forced herself to get out of the car and headed inside to talk to Evan. It wasn't like he was even unreasonable, but she'd never tested the idea of a temporary separation on him.

Zoe was being foolish. She had to get this out in the open because the truth was she needed help. She needed to figure out what to do. She couldn't do anything until Evan knew. She couldn't make plans. She couldn't accept the internship. She couldn't talk to her mom. She could do nothing until she talked to Evan, figured out the plan and that was the honest truth.

The jingle of the bell overhead as she opened the door to the hardware store had always given her joy. She loved Evan. She loved Evan more than she loved life itself, didn't she? Yes. She did. Why was she being so stupid about this? Well, that stopped now.

She didn't see any customers, so she called out her husband's name. "Evan?" Zoe walked toward the counter where the register was. She expected him to pop up from behind the counter, flashing her his ever-present smile because he loved his hardware store. He loved working here, he loved what he'd created and he was proud of himself. He should be, because he worked very hard to make this business a success.

Zoe was so proud of him. It was very quiet in the hardware store today, which was odd.

"Evan?" She walked past the register, which was centrally located towards the back where the employees-only entry was. It led to the back room and the storage area. Just as she reached for the doorknob to push inside to the back area, the door popped open and one of Evan's employees stopped short.

"Mrs. Pierce, what are you doing here?" Tyler asked. He was a high school student that Evan had hired for the summer, but Tyler only went to school half days for some reason and worked here in the afternoons. Since it was still morning, it must be a school holiday of some sort.

"Hi ,Tyler," Zoe said. "I was little worried when I came in here and there was nobody around."

"Oh, yeah, I had to go take a—well, I mean, um…" Tyler's face suddenly turned a vivid shade of crimson and Zoe realized he'd probably been to the bathroom. She only hoped he'd washed his hands.

Zoe changed the subject quickly by asking, "Where's Evan? I just stopped in real quick to ask him a question."

Tyler cleared his throat and gave an exaggerated nod. "Oh ,yeah, Mr. Pierce is in the back unloading a trailer. We had an order come in early so he asked if I could come in today and cover the front. Today's some sort of teacher conference or something, I don't know. Anyway, it's a day off for me. Well, I mean not off, since I had to come in to work, I guess." His expression changed to one of confusion, but Zoe was in a hurry.

"Thanks, Tyler. I'll find Evan on my own." Zoe brushed past the youth, knowing that if she didn't leave he'd keep talking and stammering until the moon was out and stars twinkled in the night sky.

"Okay, Mrs. Pierce. Nice talking to you." Tyler was a very nice boy, but really talkative.

Zoe didn't respond except to send a finger wave over one shoulder as she kept moving toward the small loading dock at the back of the building. It led out into the alley behind the Evan's store. The loading dock door was closed, so Zoe opened the regular door next to it wide enough that she could lean out and look for Evan.

She saw him with a clipboard in hand, bent over reading the paper on it, making a few checks with his pen, as he nodded occasionally and chatted with the truck driver.

Zoe called out, "Evan?"

The truck driver saw her first, peeking over Evan's shoulder. He lifted his ball cap in salute. Zoe waved at him as her husband half turned and looked in her direction. The moment he saw her, he grinned like he was the luckiest man in the world and waved at her.

For some reason, Zoe's eyes teared up. She was glad he was too far away to see her eyes water, because he would want to know why immediately before anything else.

Evan loved her. She knew this to be true. And Zoe loved him. She should have already told him her big news. She kicked herself for being worried over this internship issue. She didn't know how yet, but somehow they would work it out. She just knew it. Maybe it wouldn't even be an issue at all. At least she hoped so.

Evan said a few words to the truck driver that she didn't hear. When they both laughed out loud, she figured he was making some comment about being married or having a wife or the old adage, "happy wife, happy life." They shook hands before parting. The truck driver took a piece of paper from Evan and climbed up into his cab, waving out the window as he drove off.

Zoe watched her gorgeous husband walk across the parking lot, up the stairs and through the door to where she stood. He had his arms around her and his lips pressed to her mouth before she could say a word. She wrapped her arms around his shoulders, leaned into his kiss and counted herself the luckiest girl in the world.

"I love you, Zoe," he said. But then he didn't let her respond before kissing her again.

Zoe finally lifted her head, breaking the lovely kiss and said, "I need to talk to you about something. I've sort of been putting it off."

Evan pulled away slightly and she saw the concern shaping his face. "Oh? What's up?"

Zoe took a deep breath and said, "Quite a while ago, before we even started dating, I applied for an internship. I didn't expect to get it because there were like a thousand applicants or something. Anyway, for some reason they offered it to me."

Evan listened and then a sudden smile shaped his mouth. "But that's awesome! Good for you, Zoe. I'm so proud of you. Why did you put this off? This is great news."

Zoe straightened and separated herself from her husband. "I didn't say anything to you yet because, well, because this internship is out of town."

"You mean like in Cape Canaveral Beach instead of Cape Canaveral North?"

Zoe shook her head. "No. I mean like Miami." She watched him absorb the word.

He blinked a few times and then cocked his head to one side. "Miami? Like Miami, Florida?"

Zoe nodded.

She closed her eyes and started talking fast. "Honestly, Evan, I never in a thousand years expected to get this internship. But it's a very prestigious. It would be foolish to turn it down. I would be a fool to turn it down. And yet I've been trying to figure out a way to tell you. Because it would be a six-month internship three and a half hours away from here. I'd have to live there. And I don't even know if you can visit." *Please don't be mad.*

When he didn't say anything, Zoe opened her eyes halfway to assess his feelings on what she'd just spouted out at rapid speed. He blinked several times as if surprised.

However, Evan did not do what Zoe expected. She expected him to frown and grumble and say he didn't want her to go to Miami or any number of things that would be the expected reaction to his wife of a very short time planning to leave him for six months for an internship in a busy city. But instead of grumbling or being angry, he laughed.

In fact, he laughed so long and so hard that he bent over, put his hands on his knees and laughed some more.

Zoe was concerned. Why was he laughing? "What is so funny? What is wrong with you?"

"I'm sorry, honey." Evan straightened up, turned to her and put both of his palms on her shoulders, squeezing gently as he looked deeply into her eyes. "The thing is I've been trying to get up the nerve to tell you something, as well."

"What do you want to tell me?" Zoe didn't know what in the world was going on.

"Do you remember this morning when I ran out of the house like my butt was on fire?"

Zoe shrugged. "I was too busy sneaking around upstairs trying to be quiet hoping you'd already left for work. I found some courage and was about to tell you about the internship when I guess you *did* run out pretty fast this morning."

"I was afraid you'd figured out *my* big secret and I didn't want to talk about it yet."

"What big secret? What are you talking about? You have something to tell me?"

Evan nodded. He gently took both of her hands in his. "You know the new company that I just agreed to work with to provide parts for their statewide stores? Guess where they are headquartered."

Zoe narrowed her eyes. "Could it possibly be...Miami?!"

"Yes! It is Miami! You're the winner! And you have just won a trip to beautiful, busy, hot Miami! With your husband, whether you want to go with him or not!"

"You're going to Miami? When?" Zoe was flabbergasted. She felt like she was on a rollercoaster ride. Here she'd been so worried for days for nothing.

"Oh, in a couple of months or so. So when are *you* going to Miami?"

"Once I gratefully accept the internship— which I haven't even done yet— I'll be leaving in a couple of months or so." Zoe threw her arms around Evan's neck and squeezed. She kissed his face repeatedly and wished she hadn't been so foolish about telling her husband what was bothering her.

"You should've seen your face. Best shock-face ever," Evan said.

Zoe punched him lightly in the shoulder. A huge weight had just flown off her shoulders when her husband told her he was also going to Miami for business. She didn't know how long he was going for, but it didn't matter because it looked like they'd be going together. That news was amazing. Whatever issues and troubles they might have, she knew they would work them out. Now the only problem she had was figuring out how to tell her mother about the internship in Miami.

"I'm sorry I didn't tell you right away. I didn't want to be separated from you for six whole months. But I really wanted to take this internship."

"I'm sorry, too, Zoe," he said. "I say we make a pact and from now on we tell each other everything, no matter how bad we think it will be."

"I agree. Pact accepted."

"Good. I was about to grow an ulcer when I found out they wanted me to spend a few months down in Miami, learning their logistics system and what was expected of me and the like. I mean it's a lot of money they are spending, so they want me to be trained and understand all their systems. I just didn't know how I was going to leave you behind."

"Okay, so now that I don't feel like I have to turn down the awesome internship that I really wanted my only problem is telling my mom. She was counting on me to not only be around for the next eight months to help out with the renovations, I think she's expecting me to intern with her.

"How do I tell her that I will *not* be interning at the Driftwood Inn or with *your* mother at the Lighthouse Inn, but that I'm leaving her to deal with an expansion mostly on her own?"

Evan nodded with an understanding expression, but she could tell he was thinking about something, too.

"What are you thinking? Please tell me something good that will help me."

"Well, I was thinking that maybe if we talk to my mom, then perhaps she can help break the news to your mom in a softer way. What do you think?"

Zoe pushed out a sigh of relief. "I think that's a marvelous idea."

"Good. We'll go talk to my mom first, because I'm going to ask her if she can kinda help watch over my hardware store while I'm gone for the next three or four months. Although it might be better if she's available to help your mother at the inn. She does have experience and can provide references if necessary." Evan smiled.

"I know for a fact she's probably overqualified, but can she do both? Watch your store and also help my mom?"

Evan's brows furrowed. That probably meant no, not likely.

"I have an idea."

"What?"

"Why don't you ask your brother-in-law, Derek Covington, to help out with your hardware store, too? Maybe he and your mother could rotate days."

Evan's face brightened in an instant. "That is a great idea. Thanks, Zoe. I'll call him later today." He squeezed both her hands and added, "You know, Zoe, I think your mom is going to be proud of you. She will miss you, of course, but I don't think for a minute that she'll be upset."

"Do you really think so? I hate to leave her in the lurch with this expansion coming when she was sort of counting on me to help her out over the next eight months."

"I really believe that. She will be proud of you. She will be delighted that you're going to be the recipient of a prestigious internship in Miami and I know my mom will be proud of you, too."

"Thank you so much. Honestly, I don't know why it took me so long to tell you this. You are my friend. Even if you weren't going to Miami, too, you wouldn't have been mad at me or told me not to go."

He laughed. "No. I promise I would not have been mad at you. I'm very proud of you."

"Well, from now on I'll just tell you instead of hoping that you will read my mind."

"I vow to do the same thing," Evan said, raising one hand in the air as if he were swearing on a Bible in court. "From this day forward, with the vows we spoke at the courthouse, regarding in sickness and in health, etcetera, we shall also add with good news or bad news, doesn't matter. We talk to each other. Right?"

"Right," she said.

Zoe and Evan hugged again, gently swaying back and forth, each trying to settle their nerves from the almost-argument they both expected to have.

Life was good. Life with Evan was very good. Life in Miami was going to be crazy and disruptive to their normal lives, but at least they were going to do this trip together.

When they spoke to Evan's mother late that day, she had to admit that Evan had been right on the money. Roberta Pierce had been very proud of both Zoe and Evan and had agreed to not only soften the blow with Miranda if needed, but also to pitch in to cover Evan's store while he was gone. She also said Miranda would be so excited that Zoe got such a prestigious internship, she was certain she wouldn't have to soften the blow at all.

When Evan called Derek to tell him about their plans to live in Miami for a few months, Derek had wholeheartedly offered lend a hand at Evan's hardware store. He also offered the use of several trusted employees to help as well. Evan was set for his trip south.

When they went to talk to Zoe's mother, she looked a bit sad, like she'd been crying. Zoe almost turned around and left. However, her mom invited them both in to chat.

"Don't worry, dear. I just had a bit of a long day. I'll tell you about it later, okay? Now, what's up, Zoe? You look flushed."

Zoe looked at Evan for moral support and then turned to her mother. "I have some pretty big news. And I'm just going to say it. My college professor told me this week that I was awarded the Ritz-Carleton Biscayne Bay, Miami internship."

Her mother's eyes widened to the size of saucers. She put both hands to her face and tears gushed out of her eyes and rolled down her cheeks. Zoe was about to say she was sorry, but her mother, said, "That's amazing, Zoe! I'm so proud of you." Her hands dropped from her face, she stood up and she grabbed Zoe in a big hug. "I can't believe it. How long do you get to go for? You know, I've heard that some interns have gone on to get permanent jobs after being in that program." Her mother screamed in excitement.

"I was so worried you'd be mad."

"Mad? Why would I be mad?" her mother asked, seemingly not understanding what it meant for the Driftwood Inn.

"Because I have to be gone for six months when you are renovating."

"Oh, don't worry about that, my darling. I'll be just fine. I've been doing this bed-and-breakfast gig for a while now. I'm sorry you thought I'd be upset, and of course I'll miss you, my sweet Zoe, but this is big news. So, is it okay if I tell everyone I know? I'm a proud mother and I must brag."

Zoe laughed. "Sure. Tell the whole world, but start tomorrow. I need to hand in my official acceptance."

Her mother looked at Evan. "Are you okay with Zoe being gone for so long?"

Evan grinned. "Well, actually, I also have some news." He told her all about his new business venture with the trucking company, and how he and Zoe would be together for several months in Miami. He added that even if he hadn't had this big opportunity, he would still have been very proud of Zoe and supported her Miami internship.

"I would have brought you food so you wouldn't starve," Miranda told him.

"Good to know," Evan said. "I can barely boil water."

"Oh, that's not true. You can boil water...and that's about it."

Zoe was so relieved. It looked like she would continue on with her happily ever after with Evan after all.

Epilogue

Beverly slung her purse over one shoulder and walked across the parking lot of the Cape Canaveral North Beachside Supermarket after her husband had her car towed right out from under her. She was either going to have to call a taxi, an Uber or family member whenever she was ready to leave the grocery store.

She wandered the aisles for a while, haphazardly tossing stuff into the cart. Then, standing in the frozen foods section, she realized Noah must've had her car fitted with a GPS tracker. How else would he have known to send the tow-truck driver to the grocery store?

Beverly didn't know where she'd been going after she left her mother's house. The revenge plan to spend quite a lot of money on a dinner she knew he probably wouldn't eat hadn't come to her until she was driving away from the Driftwood Inn.

She wondered how long the GPS tracker had been on her car. Had it been there the whole time they'd been married? Or was this only a recent addition, since she'd left him and spent a couple of days at her sister's house two months ago. Had

Noah known then that their marriage was doomed to fail? Was that why he'd been treating her so poorly for the last two months? Had he just been biding his time, waiting for her to finally say enough?

Beverly started walking down the aisle once more. She was grateful that the Beachside Supermarket was fairly quiet. As she strolled past aisle six, where baby food, diapers and, oddly enough, picnic supplies were stocked, she noticed a man standing in the center of the aisle staring at little jars of baby food.

She kept walking until she made the circuit back to the frozen foods section, did an about-face, and walked back along the main aisle of the grocery store. When she passed by aisle six, the man was still standing there. He had moved slightly, and this time she noticed he had a very small baby strapped to his chest in a harness-like contraption that was all the rage.

As Beverly walked by, a smile shaped her face. Was there anything sweeter than a big, burly, handsome man with a teeny tiny baby strapped to his chest? No. She thought not. Because that was pretty sweet.

She glanced at her watch, wondering how long she was going to keep walking back and forth along the main aisle of the grocery store. If she'd been wearing her exercise tracker, she would've already gotten her daily steps in. Alas, her exercise tracker was back at home. Or rather, the home she was probably about to be kicked out of.

She walked past aisle six for a third time, where the man stood like a statue. The baby had started to fuss. Apparently, the noise of a crying baby, which really sounded like a teeny tiny mewling kitten, had not registered on the new father. He stood there, staring a tiny jars of baby food, as if he thought they would tell him what he should buy and leap into his arms, ready to be purchased. She hated to break it to him, but that was not about to happen.

Beverly left her cart and walked slowly towards the man in aisle six. He looked a little familiar, although she wasn't sure where she could possibly have seen him. He was easily over six feet tall, he had dark hair with some wave to it. He could probably leap out of bed, finger-comb his hair and go on about his day looking perfect.

She could only see his profile. It was enough to notice he was very good-looking. With his chiseled features and angular jaw, he would make any male model jealous. His clothes were very nice and he certainly filled them out well. But he was dressed casually in jeans with a collared shirt that sort of reminded her of when Noah would dress down.

The only time she'd ever seen him do it was for a neighborhood barbecue, and then she'd never seen him do it again. He had definitely not been a fan of casual clothing. But Beverly didn't have to worry about know anymore. He could burn all of his casual clothes for all she cared. Taking her car away and leaving her stranded and embarrassing her was a bridge too far. Even if he did want her back or if he didn't kick her out tonight, she was leaving. Good riddance to bad rubbish.

"Excuse me," Beverly said in a low tone. "Are you okay?"

The man didn't move for a few seconds, then startled as if he'd just come out of a trance.

"I'm sorry, what did you say?" he asked.

"I asked if you're okay. I'm having a pretty awful day and I've been pacing back and forth along the main aisle of this grocery store for a while. I happened to notice you seemed to be a little out of your depth, if you don't mind me saying so."

He did look really familiar. "My name is Beverly Peyton. Have we met before?"

The man went to stick his right hand out as if to shake hers and introduce himself, noticed a diaper bag was clenched in his fist. For an instant he looked positively horrified, then he laughed. "I am also having a pretty awful day," he said. "You look familiar to me, too, but I have absolutely no idea where I know you from."

When she'd said her last name was Peyton, she had sort of expected some recognition, but he did not seem to know the Peyton name. That was a point in his favor as far as Beverly was concerned.

"I'm Alec Varden. Pleased to meet you, Beverly." He looked down at the baby strapped to his chest, and added, "This is my baby, Claire."

Claire was becoming rather fretful. Beverly stepped closer and said, "May I help soothe her? I'm pretty good with babies."

Alec nodded. "That would be fantastic, because I'm hopeless with babies."

Beverly helped get Claire out of the contraption strapped to Alec's chest and cradled the tiny baby. She stopped crying the minute she was secure in Beverly's arms. She rocked back and forth and stared down into the bluest eyes she'd seen in a while. Claire was adorable.

"Wow. You *are* good with babies. I don't suppose you're looking for a job as a nanny, are you?"

Beverly almost answered with, "No, I'm not looking for a job." Then she thought about it. She hadn't been looking for a job, until her car had been towed out from under her. Tonight, she was planning on sneaking back into her own home to gather a few of her personal items. So she was not in the mood to pooh-pooh a job offer. "I might be interested," Beverly said. "Are you joking? Or do you really need a nanny?"

"I really am looking for a nanny, right this minute, as a matter of fact." Alec looked at her closely again as she rocked back and forth, holding his sweet baby Claire in her arms. "You remind me of the owner of the Driftwood Inn. Do you know Miranda Cole?"

Beverly laughed out loud, but quietly, so as not to disturb the baby, who was about to fall asleep. "I do know her. She's my mother."

Alec said, "Your mother is a lovely woman. I guess you know that. Both she and I were on a charity auction board a few years back. I believe we still hold the record for the most money earned in a single year."

"Yes. My mother is a very lovely woman, thank you so much for saying that. I do remember her being on that charity auction board. That's probably why you look so familiar to me."

"I have to tell you that I'm serious about needing a nanny in a most desperate way. If you are interested, would you like to start right now. If not now, how about tomorrow."

"The truth is, I could start right now," Beverly said. "However, I feel the need to be honest with you, as well, about where I am in my life right now." She told him a condensed version of how she'd married in haste a man who no longer wanted to be married to her. That he had just had her car towed.

And that if he wasn't completely horrified by her current life story, would he be so kind as to drop her off at the Driftwood Inn, because otherwise she would have to walk there.

She also told him she would be delighted to start working as baby Claire's nanny. "If you're truly interested in hiring me, name the time and I will be there."

Alex said, "I'm very sorry for your troubles, however, I am grateful that you want to work for me as a nanny. Therefore, you're hired. If you could be at my house by tomorrow morning at, say, 9 a.m., that would be awesome."

Beverly continued to sway back and forth, even though baby Claire had fallen asleep a few minutes ago. "All I need is your address. And also a phone number would probably be a good idea. I would give you my phone number, but I suspect my husband is about to close my account down."

Alec lifted his head and looked in the direction of the front of the store. "I'll tell you what—I'll buy you a burner phone. It's the least I can do since you got my baby to stop crying. I'm really hoping that you will carry her all the way out to the car and put her in the car seat that was hellish to get her into the last time. Also, if you could help me figure out what she will eat, I would be eternally grateful.

Beverly nodded. "I'm delighted to help you do all those things. And I can actually buy my own burner phone, which sounds very clandestine and I like it. Maybe I can be your super-secret nanny. How cool would that be?"

"That would be very cool. Is there anything you need to buy here, besides the burner phone?"

Beverly had come to the grocery store on a revenge mission, had her car taken away from her, been humiliated by her soon-to-be ex-husband, had done several laps through the aisles, found a man clearly in worse shape than she was, and suddenly had a job, a sweet baby to care for, and new hope on her horizon.

She thought it was a shame that Alec's wife had left him. She'd heard stories about terrible postpartum symptoms for women right after they'd had a baby, but she'd never personally known anyone who had experienced it.

Beverly would gladly be a nanny to sweet baby Claire and for Alec, but if his wife did come back, she would certainly step aside and be understanding about moving on. Sometimes people just needed some time to sort things out. She better than anyone understood how that worked. She'd been trying to sort things out for years, trying to learn how to get along with the Peyton family, but resisting their demands that become a snooty snob like they were.

Now she was free of all that nonsense.

All in all, it had been quite a day for Beverly. She was toting a beautiful newborn baby around, she had a new job opportunity, she was about to buy a clandestine burner phone and, for the first time in a long time, she felt good about herself. She was helping someone. For all that time she spent pacing the aisles, the truth was she didn't know where to go or what to do. Everything she thought of seemed like the wrong thing, like it was the coward's way out or simply impossible to make happen.

So for the time being, Beverly decided things were looking up. She had hope for her future. She was going to hate having to give the baby back, but at least she got to see Claire tomorrow morning. She just truly wanted this feeling of hopefulness to last for a long time.

It had been quite a long time since she had felt wanted and needed.

Beverly had missed this warm feeling of instant acceptance. She refused to let it go.

She smiled up at Alec, cupped her hand protectively on the back of baby Claire's head, and said, "Where did you see those burner phones?"

Next in the series will be: Driftwood Dreams, Cape Canaveral North, book 2.

About The Author

Amy Ashley

 Amy Ashley has always lived on the East Coast because she loves the ocean and the beach. She never strays too far away as both the salt tang in the air and the sensation of sand squishing between her toes gives her joy.

If not strolling along the shoreline searching for shells, she's cooking, reading or spending time with her hubby, her daughters and a spoiled beagle named, Scout.

Books By This Author

The Lighthouse Inn: Cape Canaveral Beach Complete Series

Take a trip to Florida's East Coast and enjoy the sandy shores of Cape Canaveral Beach. The Pierce family must navigate the challenges of life after losing their much-loved patriarch, and where better to do that than on vacation at The Lighthouse Inn, the family's lovely B&B.

A year after her husband's sudden death in a diving accident, Roberta Pierce is doing her best to move on with her lonely, retired life in Key West. Each day gets better, but she still misses Charlie terribly. She hopes a visit to Cape Canaveral Beach, the Lighthouse Inn and, of course, her four children -- Beth, Evan, Emily and Erin -- will raise her spirits. But Roberta soon discovers that even though they're adults, her children still need her support, advice and guidance to navigate their surprisingly challenging and demanding lives.

Beth Pierce Weller, Roberta's eldest daughter, runs

the Lighthouse Inn with her husband Randy. But there's trouble in paradise and only Roberta can help Beth get through it.

Evan Pierce runs his own hardware store. When he's not helping customers, he stays busy dodging his mother's match-making attempts. Evan swears he's too busy for love. But is he? A surprise meeting one night might change his mind.

Emily Pierce is working hard to open a bakery in town, a dream she's had since childhood. But she's underestimated the investment this start-up business will take. When Emily's money runs out before the bakery opens, she makes an awful mistake. She should 'fess up, but she can't find the courage to tell anyone the terrible trouble she's in. Not even her fiancé, Luke Calder, who harbors secrets of his own. Emily trusted one of her mother's friends after he offered to help her out. Turns out, not only isn't he a friend, he's pestering her every day. Can her mother even help her at this point?

Erin Pierce is a college student in her final year, anxious to finish her education and get on with her life. At 21, she's already in love with the perfect man. Too bad he's her brother's arch business rival. What will happen when Evan – or, heaven forbid, her mother – discovers that Erin has fallen for the son of the man thought to be responsible for her father's death?

With all the troubles her children face, Roberta clearly has her work cut out for her. She rolls up her sleeves, determined to save her family from themselves. But when love comes knocking at Roberta's door a second time, will she be too involved in solving her children's problems to answer?

Made in the USA
Columbia, SC
29 September 2021